The Missing Ingredient

MYSTERY
and the
MINISTER'S
WIFE

The Missing Ingredient

DIANE NOBLE

GUIDEPOSTS
NEW YORK, NEW YORK

The Missing Ingredient

ISBN-13: 978-0-8249-4821-4

Published by Guideposts
16 East 34th Street
New York, New York 10016
www.guideposts.com

Distributed by Ideals Publications, a Guideposts company
2630 Elm Hill Pike, Suite 100
Nashville, Tennessee 37214

The author is represented by the literary agency of Alive Communications, Inc.,
7680 Goddard Street, Suite 200, Colorado Springs, Colorado 80920.

Library of Congress Cataloging-in-Publication Data

Noble, Diane, 1945-
The missing ingredient / Diane Noble.
    p. cm. — (Mystery and the minister's wife)
ISBN 978-0-8249-4821-4
1. Spouses of clergy—Fiction. 2. Clergy—Fiction. 3. Television cooking shows—
Fiction. 4. Celebrity chefs—Fiction. 5. City and town life—Tennessee—Fiction.
I. Title.
PS3563.A3179765M57 2010
813'.54—dc22

2010007867

Cover by Lookout Design Group
Interior design by Cris Kossow
Typeset by Aptara

Printed and bound in the United States of America

10 9 8 7 6 5 4 3 2 1

To Barbara Doyle
"I breathed a song into the air,
It fell to earth, I knew not where;
For who has sight so keen and strong
That it can follow the flight of song?
Long, long afterward . . .
The song, from beginning to end,
I found again in the heart of a friend."
(A paraphrase of "The Arrow and the Song"
by Henry Wadsworth Longfellow)

You helped me find my song, dear Barbara.

Chapter One

Dusk was closing in fast, and a mist had wrapped itself around the trees, eerily hugging the ground. Kate maneuvered her black Honda into the parking lot and came to a halt in front of the Hamilton Springs Hotel. She looked up at the two-story brick building and told herself that her trepidation about being near the property was pure nonsense.

But what if the author of *Famous Haunts of the South* was right?

The Hamilton Springs, a haunted hotel? She chuckled. She knew better, of course. Even so, she couldn't help glancing at the windows in the wing where the ghost was said to roam. She also couldn't help the shiver that slid down her spine.

She turned off the ignition and stepped out of the car just as Livvy and Danny Jenner pulled up beside her, followed by Renee Lambert and her mother, Caroline Beauregard Johnston, in a pink Oldsmobile.

A few seconds later, Eli Weston swung his truck into the parking lot and glided to a stop on the far side of Kate's Honda. Car after car pulled in, and soon enough, a lively, chattering

group of a half-dozen others from around town—LuAnne
Matthews, Millie Lovelace, Sam Gorman, Willy Bergen, and
Joe Tucker—gathered in the lot. Lucy Mae Briddle stood by,
notebook and pen in hand. She had recently been hired to run
the front office of the *Copper Mill Chronicle* and had been trying her hand at reporting recently.

Joe Tucker? Kate grinned and waved. A lean and wizened
backwoodsman, Joe was one of the last citizens of Copper
Mill she expected to see come out to greet the celebrity chefs
of the Taste Network.

She tried not to show her surprise as the group trotted
over to join her. But Joe had a knack for reading people before
they said a word.

He leaned on his hand-carved walking stick, crossed one
foot over the other, and chuckled. "You didn't know about my
cookin', did you? I don't put much stock in television, but I've
taken to watchin' the Taste channel recently. Learned how to
make the best oyster-turkey stuffing you'd ever want to lap a
lip over. Learned it from one of the Taste gals—Birdie Birge
—last Thanksgiving. I wouldn't miss this for the world."

The others chimed in, all talking at once. Kate picked up
snatches of "new recipes for the diner" from LuAnne and
Loretta; "been into gourmet food lately" from Eli; "thought I
might find something for the Civil War reenactments" from
Willy; "love chocolate and thought *why not?*" from Millie; and
"just thought it'd be fun" from Sam, with a sheepish grin and a
shrug.

"Tonight's the big night, all right." Renee headed around
the back of Kate's Honda to join the group. Kisses, on a jeweled

111112

leash, trailed behind. "Can you believe they're actually coming to Copper Mill?"

Caroline brought up the rear. "Who, the ghosts?" she snorted.

"Now, Mother, you know good and well what I mean. The Taste Network. The celebrity chefs, film crew, producers, directors—the whole enchilada!"

But Caroline didn't appear to be listening. She was peering suspiciously at the same wing of the hotel Kate had taken in earlier. Kate thought she saw a shudder travel up Caroline's spine, and she understood the older woman's apprehension. Darkness was rapidly turning the landscape a shadowy gray, and moisture from the heavy mist now dripped from the trees. Street lights cast an eerie glow around the parking lot before being swallowed up by the foggy night.

A hush seemed to crawl over the parking lot. They had all obviously heard the new rumors about a ghost in the Hamilton Springs Hotel.

Even Kisses sensed something otherworldly. Facing the hotel, the little Chihuahua put his ears back and growled. No matter how Renee tried to distract him, he kept it up. Kate noticed he was trembling all over. But then, he did that even under the most ordinary circumstances.

LuAnne glanced around with a nervous expression. "I thought the trucks would be here by now. I hope we don't have to stand out here too long. It's cold."

"They're not all trucks. Some are called star coaches," Renee corrected with a sniff. "All the stars have them. There will be three—one for each of the big-name chefs: Birdie Birge, Nicolette Pascal, and Susannah Applebaum."

"So they stay in their coaches instead of the hotel?" Livvy asked.

"The star coaches are just for travel." Renee's tone implied this was information everyone should know. "Sometimes they have beds for naps and furniture for relaxing while they travel."

A brisk breeze stung Kate's face, and she rubbed her hands together to warm them. "I say we all go inside and wait. As soon as the network people get here, we'll head back out to greet the celebrities, just like we planned."

Renee narrowed her eyes at the hotel. "Never thought I'd see the day I'd be reluctant to step inside the Hamilton Springs. I consider all this ghost business as folderol, but there's something eerie about this night. . . ."

There were murmurs of agreement from the women. The men didn't seem too worried, though Joe Tucker, looking solemn and wise, didn't utter a word one way or the other.

Danny Jenner chuckled. "Folderol is right. I don't for a minute believe in any of this nonsense. The hotel's perfectly safe."

"I wonder why there have been so few guests lately," Loretta Sweet said, scanning the hotel windows with their noticeably few lights. "I bet it's because of that new *Famous Haunts of the South* book." She shook her head slowly. "I can almost see the ghost of Precious McFie walking by those windows in her wedding gown. No wonder people are staying away." She paused, then went on in a whisper. "It's said she haunts the hotel, the parking lot, and the path along the creek. I sorta wish I hadn't read that book. Keeps me awake at night."

Livvy stepped up to stand beside Kate. "You can talk all

about it with the author," she said to the others, "on Saturday night. He'll be at the library for a book signing and Q and A."

"I read about that in the *Chronicle*," Renee said with a scowl. "Not so sure that's a good idea—getting him to come here, I mean."

"Of course, it's a good idea," Caroline snorted. "It's about time we got a big-time author to come to town. Besides, I like his name—Joel St. Nicklaus. Though I plan to tell him that he should've written a book about the ghosts of Christmas past, not the ones that haunt the South."

The others chuckled, but no one pointed out that the author's name wasn't spelled the same as the Saint Nicholas of Santa Claus fame.

"Why don't you think it's a good idea?" Eli asked Renee.

She shrugged. "People are grumbling about it already, and having the author here will just make it worse. Some believe in ghosts; others don't. I was having pie and coffee at the diner the other day and heard a shouting match in a booth across the room. It all had to do with ghosts."

LuAnne nodded. "I waited on that group. Started out good-natured, then some of them got to talkin' about personal experiences." She shivered. "Got pretty spooky too."

"Real ghosts, you mean?" Millie asked, her eyes wide.

"Yep, real as flesh and bone," she said. "At least, that's how they were talkin'."

Danny chuckled. "*Flesh and bone* might not be the operative words here."

Millie let out a shaky sigh. "I don't even want to think about that." She fell silent for a moment, then added, "Some of our Faith Briar folks are up in arms. People have been calling

Pastor Paul to get his opinion about ghosts and hauntings and all that." Millie was the church secretary at Faith Briar.

Kate sighed. The phone had been ringing off the hook at the parsonage too. Nearly everyone was asking the same question: "Are there really ghosts?"

"Who all called?" Renee was suddenly more interested than before. "And what did the pastor tell them?"

Millie had the grace to simply raise an eyebrow. She might be difficult at times, but she could also be trusted to keep conversations and church business confidential.

A cold wind blew across the parking lot, and for a brief instant, the fingers of fog seemed to engage in some sort of eerie dance. Even Danny Jenner looked startled.

"The ghost. I'm just sure that's why nobody else showed up," LuAnne said in a hushed voice. "Word's gettin' out that the whole place is haunted."

"I say," Kate broke in, "we all go into the foyer and warm up by the fire—"

"Wait!" Willy cupped his ear with his hand. "Do you hear that?"

"What?" Millie and LuAnne said in unison.

"I thought I heard a chain rattle," Caroline whispered.

Millie gasped and splayed her hand over her chest.

Willy frowned. "No, no! Nothin' like that. I hear diesel engines coming down the grade. They're still a distance away, but there—there it is again." He raised an eyebrow. "Y'all hear it?"

Visible relief washed over LuAnne, Millie, Caroline, and even Renee. Livvy and Kate exchanged glances, and Kate resisted rolling her eyes.

"I hear them," Sam said. "Those are diesel trucks, all right."

The other men agreed.

The faint sounds of downshifting gears carried toward them, and Kate grinned.

"That's got to be the people from Taste," she said.

The citizens of Copper Mill seemed thrilled the network had chosen the Bristol, the restaurant attached to the Hamilton Springs Hotel, for taping its special segment *Great Chefs of the South*, but their excitement was nothing compared to Kate's.

Susannah Applebaum, one of the chefs, had been one of Kate's best friends growing up. They hadn't seen each other for years, but as soon as Kate heard that Susannah was going to be part of the cooking show—and after sleuthing her way through agents and publicists—Kate had made contact.

Susannah had been delighted to hear from Kate, and they had arranged to meet the morning after her arrival. Kate hadn't planned to come out that evening to welcome the network people, but Livvy had talked her into it. And as the grinding of gears grew louder, she felt glad to be there.

"They're getting closer." Livvy smiled knowingly.

Within a few minutes, the first of the big eighteen-wheelers pulled into the parking lot and slowed to a noisy stop. It was followed by two more, each with the Taste Network logo on the side: a top-down view of a deep-dish pie with a fancy TN stamped in the crust as if done with a pastry cutter. Then the star coaches rolled in, one for each of the three celebrity chefs, the names of their popular television shows colorfully splashed on the sides.

Behind the buses, a bright yellow Hummer rumbled into

the parking lot. There was no doubt that the man who emerged from the driver's side was someone important. Or at least *thought* he was important.

Renee pulled out her cell phone and started punching in numbers. She had made only a half-dozen calls when the townspeople started pouring into the hotel parking lot.

The Taste Network crew quickly attached floodlights to a noisy generator, lighting the mist-enshrouded parking lot like some sort of ghostly stage. The workers paid little attention to anything other than the tasks at hand—unloading equipment, unwinding electrical lines, and shouting instructions to one another.

Sybil Hudson, the general manager of the hotel, came out to greet the man who was doing most of the shouting, the same man who had arrived in the Hummer. Kate surmised that he was the one in charge. He pulled Sybil to one side, leaned in close, and wagged his finger at her, shoulders hunched as if in a permanently grumpy stance.

Even in the dim light, Kate could see the glower on Sybil's face. Whatever the man was saying appeared to upset her. After a moment, Sybil turned on her heel and stomped back into the hotel.

The man shrugged and went back to shouting at the crew.

"I'm dying to see that Birdie Birge," LuAnne said. "She's got a new book coming out; I heard about it on her show. It's called *Grits 101*." She grinned at Loretta. "The diner'll be serving up gourmet grits till the cows come home."

"It's that pretty little French cook I'm on the lookout for." Joe Tucker did a Groucho Marx impression, waving an imaginary cigar. "Don't care a thing about French cooking, but I love the way that Nicolette Pascal sashays around the kitchen."

He waggled his eyebrows as if they were as thick and bushy as Groucho's. Everyone laughed.

"*Hmmph*," Caroline said. "Isn't that just like a man? Can't see the soufflé for the sashay. Besides, she may be French, but her cooking is French fusion—French with a good old American Southern flair."

"Don't tell me I'm hearing a hint of hoopla over a celebrity chef." Renee shot her mother a "gotcha" look.

Kate sighed. She loved them both, but she wished just once they could put aside their sniping.

"My favorite is the chocolate show," Loretta said. "I've been a fan of Susannah Applebaum for years. I have all her cookbooks and can't wait for the next one—*Chocolates to Die For*." She smiled. "I'm hoping she'll autograph the books I already have."

Kate was half listening to the others as she kept an eye on the luxury coach with the name of Susannah's show written across the side in an elegant font that looked like rich, dark, melted chocolate. Appropriate, because *Sumptuous Chocolates* was the name of her show.

"There she is!" Joe called out as Nicolette Pascal emerged gracefully from her luxury coach.

"And there's the grits lady," shouted LuAnne with equal enthusiasm when Birdie Birge stepped out of her coach. "I'd know her anywhere. I've seen her dressed to kill when she does her entertaining segment."

Birdie hammed it up for the crowd, blowing kisses with both hands, calling out hellos, and shaking hands as she trotted toward the hotel entrance. She had almost reached the door when the same blustery, belligerent man Kate had earlier noticed stepped in front of Birdie, blocking her way. Birdie's demeanor changed dramatically. Obviously upset, she spouted something that seemed to irritate him further. Though Kate couldn't hear the words, it was obvious the two didn't care for each other.

"Who *is* that man?" Kate said to no one in particular. He appeared to be knocking down people's spirits like they were bowling pins.

"Him?" Renee stepped closer. "He's the producer-director. His name is Newt Keller. I read all about him in *People* magazine at the beauty parlor. They call him Mr. Taste Network. Came up with the concept, got the financial backing, and set out to give some of the other food networks a run for their money." Her eyebrow shot up. "Word has it that he's made a lot of enemies trying to move to number one in the ratings. From what they say, he's been wildly successful, though."

As if on cue, Newt Keller loudly berated one of the crew members, who shot him a glowering look before slumping away.

"Oh my," Kate said under her breath, her heart going out to the people who worked with the obviously unhappy man.

"Mr. Personality had better watch his p's and q's, if you ask me," Renee said.

The sudden rev of an engine caught Kate's attention, and she turned to see a zippy silver Mazda Miata roar into the parking lot and screech to a halt near the *Sumptuous Chocolates* star coach. Seconds later, the driver-side door of the sports car swung open. With a big wave and a grin, Susannah Applebaum bounced out.

Kate would have known her anywhere. That ready smile. That blonde bob. That round, jolly frame. It helped that Kate had followed Susannah's show on TV through the years, but even if she hadn't, she would have recognized her dear friend.

The crowd fell silent, and for the briefest instant, Kate thought it was because of Susannah's dramatic arrival.

Then she realized they weren't looking at Susannah.

"Oh my," breathed Renee, just behind her.

"Oh dear," said Livvy.

Kisses whimpered.

"I knew it," LuAnne said, her voice trembling. "I just knew it."

"Well, I never . . ." Caroline said, then swallowed audibly.

"Smoke and mirrors," Danny said, but his voice shook.

A chill came over Kate as she turned toward the hotel and, along with the cast and crew of the Taste Network and the citizens of Copper Mill, stared at the upper floor of the hotel, her mouth dropping open.

Flickering candlelight seemed to float from window to window, room to room, as if no walls existed between.

Before Kate could blink, a shadowy, veiled figure appeared just beyond the candlelight. It seemed as thin as smoke, almost translucent. Then just as quickly, it dissolved into nothing.

An audible gasp rose from the crowd.

The hotel went dark once more, and Kate told her heart to stop its wild beating.

Chapter Two

Kate drew in a cleansing breath and laughed, albeit a little shakily. "I agree with Danny," she said to the others. "Smoke and mirrors. That's all. I'm sure what we saw can be readily explained."

"Is this my Katie?" boomed a sonorous voice behind her.

Kate whirled around at the sound of Susannah's voice. Before she could get a word out, she was drawn into a bear hug.

A half second later, both women were laughing and crying.

"Has it really been almost forty years?" Kate said, wiping her eyes as she stepped back from the hug.

"How did we let so much time go by?" Susannah grabbed a tissue from a jacket pocket. She blew her nose with gusto.

"How did you know it was me? We weren't going to get together until tomorrow morning."

"I tried to call you at home on my cell. When you didn't answer, I hoped you'd be here to greet me. So I was on the lookout."

"But still," Kate continued, "how did you know what I look—"

Susannah chuckled. "After you told me about Paul being the pastor of Faith Briar Church, I looked it up on the Internet. Your picture is right there with your husband's, standing in front of that beautiful church." She put on her glasses and peered at Kate. "And I must say, your photo doesn't do you justice. You're beautiful as ever, Katie."

Kate grinned. "And you're even more gorgeous in person than on TV."

Susannah patted her hair, obviously pleased with the compliment. Then she gave Kate a soft smile. "The real beauty is in our friendship. To think we've reconnected after all these years. . . ."

Kate turned to her friends to make introductions, but the crowd had drifted toward the knots of Taste Network cast and crew as the mayor stepped to the front of the hotel and called for everyone's attention.

Susannah leaned toward Kate as they waited for Mayor Briddle to begin. "I know we were planning to take our official trip down memory lane tomorrow, but how about a cup of tea tonight?"

"I'd love that," Kate said.

"Great! By the way, I saw the lights flicker just after I drove up. Was it a power failure or the work of the hotel's ghost?"

Kate sighed. "So you've heard about *Famous Haunts of the South?*"

"As soon as I found out I was coming here, I ran out and bought it. I've got it in my suitcase, though it's not for bedtime reading."

"Too spooky?"

She grinned. "And then some."

Just then, Mayor Briddle cleared his throat. Kate and Susannah turned to watch.

Strangely, the Taste Network cast and crew seemed disgruntled, even apprehensive. Kate frowned and glanced at those standing near her. Tension weighed as heavily in the air as the mist that hugged the ground. Or was it her imagination? When the mayor asked Newt Keller to join him at the front of the hotel, several crew members exchanged smirks. A couple rolled their eyes as if they knew what was coming.

Newt stepped forward and looked out at the clusters of crew and Copper Mill folks shivering in the cold. He put on a wide, charming smile, which surprised Kate. He was a handsome man, probably in his late forties. Boyish looking, with a round face and dark hair, silvery on the sides, that was swept back in an expensive-looking style. There was something about him that screamed Hollywood, or at least what Kate imagined to be the practiced look of show-biz types. She immediately shot a prayer heavenward, asking for forgiveness for her judgmental attitude.

"Thank you, everyone, for coming out on this inclement evening to welcome the Tasties of Taste Network. Your hospitality is so appreciated. We look forward to a terrific week with you all. Each Copper Mill citizen has received a formal invitation from Taste to join us for the tapings this week, but I want to tell you in person how much we'd like for you to come.

"Our time here will be filled with food and fun, but you all are the ingredient that makes or breaks a network such as ours. If you've not seen such a production before, you may at times feel we're moving at an agonizingly slow rate, and I beg your patience. Besides the in-studio shots, we'll be working on off-site segments for TV audience interest and fascinating tidbits in and around the hotel. We're especially interested in the ghost that haunts this place, and I know our audience will be too."

The Copper Mill folks cheered and clapped. Newt smiled out at the crowd, looking cherubic.

"It's true," he said. "Now, folks, we don't want to be accused of making you all freeze to death." He laughed. "Besides, we need you to be healthy for the tapings. So I bid you farewell. Go home and get warm, and we'll get back to work." He waved, then headed back to the crew.

"Great show of his public persona," Susannah muttered.

"I thought it was a nice speech," Kate said.

"Don't be fooled. He's been to acting school, but he couldn't make it as an actor, so he and his ex-wife started Taste Network instead."

"It's been successful, so maybe it was a good choice," Kate offered.

"Hugely successful," Susannah said. "But it seems the better the ratings are, the more ratings-hungry he becomes."

"Is that what makes him so on edge?"

"On edge?" Susannah let out a deep sigh. "That's putting it mildly. The man is a marketing genius, but his people skills are sadly lacking. Sometimes I wonder how any of us can put up with him. More than once I've thought of throwing in the towel." She shrugged one shoulder. "But I need the income, so it's no more than a fleeting dream."

Kate was surprised. "You don't like what you do?"

"I love what I do, but Keller has a way of robbing a person

of creative joy." She grinned. "But I didn't mean to dump all this on you within the first ten minutes of our reunion." She laughed heartily. "I should've waited at least fifteen."

While Susannah checked into the hotel, Kate headed to Sybil's office, which was on the ground floor, just beyond the reception desk. The door was open, so she knocked on the doorjamb.

Sybil took off her glasses and gave Kate a wan smile. She was the kind of businesswoman who never seemed to age. She could have been in her forties, or even her early fifties. She was attractive, with brown hair pulled back in a no-nonsense knot at the back of her neck.

She gestured for Kate to come in. Kate had met Sybil when she and Paul first moved to Copper Mill. After the two women exchanged e-mails, Sybil had provided information that exposed the illegal practices of a corporation that coveted Faith Briar's property. Sybil was hired as general manager of the hotel soon after.

Kate hadn't had the opportunity to work with her since. But even from a distance, Kate had come to admire the woman's wit and warmth and her grace under pressure.

Her ability to deal with any situation without getting flustered was legendary. People still talked about the time a couple was relaxing in front of the fire in the foyer, chatting about the mounted buck with an impressive rack of antlers, when a live buck with an equally impressive rack wandered through the hotel entrance and stood quietly staring at what appeared to be his twin, hanging above the fireplace. The couple ran screaming through the foyer as Sybil calmly opened the front door and quietly coaxed the deer outdoors.

Another time, Kate happened to be in the tearoom when the Philpott brothers treated their mother, Enid, to afternoon tea on her birthday. No one knew she'd brought her cat, Ruffles, in a large carrier disguised as a purse. The only problem was, she had forgotten to completely zip up the opening, and Ruffles escaped, leaping across tables, feline fur flying, pulling off linen tablecloths, sending china clattering and shattering to the floor.

It was Sybil who calmed the frantic cat, who'd climbed the drapes and roosted atop the valance, growling and spitting at anyone who came near, including Enid and her sons. Sybil ordered the waiter to bring her a tin of tuna and a can opener. Within thirty seconds, a purring Ruffles descended the drapes and willingly entered the carrier.

Then Sybil calmed the disgruntled guests with offers of extra desserts and went table to table pouring fresh tea.

It was also rumored that she could get along with anyone, whether everyday hotel guests or bigwigs from the corporate office. Everyone seemed to love Sybil, and as far as Kate knew, Sybil treated everyone with the same respect and affection.

That's what made it all the more surprising for Kate to see Sybil's red-rimmed eyes, her agitated demeanor, her pale face and shaking hands.

Then it hit her. Newt Keller.

Sybil reached for a tissue and blew her nose. "I'm sorry," she said, blinking rapidly. "I don't know what's come over me."

"Was it the producer?" Kate ventured gently, taking a seat across from Sybil. "I noticed you talking with him earlier."

Sybil frowned briefly, then shook her head. "He's . . ." Her voice drifted off. "Well, let's just say he's going to be a challenge to work with." She sniffed and reached for another tissue. "He wants to capitalize on the rumors about the Hamilton Springs ghost. When I said no and tried to explain why, he said I didn't have the right to stop him. He's already arranged to interview experts on haunted houses and ghosts in a special segment of the show."

"Oh dear," Kate said.

"It gets worse. He's calling the special segment 'Ten Reasons to Avoid Staying in a Haunted Hotel.'" She blinked at Kate. "Can you imagine that? He told me it's supposed to be 'tongue in cheek,' and the audience will 'get it.' Those were his exact words. He's even planning to tell his audience that the hotel once had to close because of ghost activity, and I'm sure he'll mention that he wonders if it will happen again."

Kate sat forward, her eyes widening. "Was it? Closed, I mean, because of ghost activity?"

"Yes, in the fifties. Guests stayed away to the point where the hotel almost went under."

"People find oddities like this interesting. Maybe the publicity will be good for the hotel," Kate said. "Maybe it will become even better known than it is now."

Sybil shook her head. "That's the kind of publicity we don't need. This is a grand old hotel, renovated four-star-plus, all the way. Our guests expect a certain kind of understated elegance, not a foyer full of ghost hunters from la-la land."

"Speaking of ghosts, did you see the . . . ah, apparition in the window tonight?"

Sybil stared at her evenly, then said, "I didn't need to. Guests have reported the same strange flicker of lights for several weeks now. They've also told me about furniture that seems to move across a room of its own accord, drapes that blow as if in the wind, though the window isn't open . . ." Her words fell off, and her face went pale with her next words. "When I get such reports, I go immediately to the rooms where the ghost activity was reported to have happened"—she reached for another tissue—"but nothing's there. Nothing at all. Nothing but a frigid air that seems to move around the room independently."

Kate blinked. "It sounds like you believe the Hamilton Springs really is haunted?"

Sybil didn't answer, but Kate could see by her expression that something was troubling her deeply. Kate sighed and leaned back in her chair. "Would you mind if I had a look around to see for myself?"

"It won't do you any good," Sybil said. "I was up there earlier and checked all the rooms. They're empty except for stored furniture, industrial cleaners, paper goods, extra linens, and such."

"Even so," Kate said, "let me look around, see if I spot something."

For a moment, the only sound in the room was the ticking of an antique clock on the credenza behind her.

Finally, Sybil spoke. "That chill I mentioned. It's like some sort of taunting wind, unlike anything I've felt before. Even the housekeepers have noticed it." She hesitated briefly, then added, "It has a personality."

"Personality?"

"Like a person, only I know logically it isn't."

"Or like a ghost," Kate whispered, imagining that the chill had blown into the room with them. "Have you seen these things yourself?"

Sybil gave her a steady look, and again, Kate noticed the pallor of her skin. Obviously unwilling to talk about it, Sybil stood, a signal that their meeting was over. "Stop by in the morning, and I'll have the key card waiting for you."

Kate stood and shook Sybil's hand. It was icy cold.

TWENTY MINUTES LATER, Kate was sitting across from Susannah in the tearoom, which was attached to the Bristol. It was nearly eight o'clock, and the room was almost empty. Susannah ordered tiramisu for them to share, and it was quickly brought to their table with a pot of Earl Grey, a small pitcher of thick cream, and a bowl of sugar cubes. She then proceeded to rate the dessert as if it were fine wine.

"Ahh," she breathed, closing her eyes. "Very nice. I taste fresh mascarpone, Black Forest kirschwasser, and a hint of almond extract. And I would guess the chef made his lady-fingers from scratch. I hereby pronounce his creation 'heaven in the mouth.'"

Kate took a bite, slowly savoring each flavor. Somewhere in the filing cabinet of her mind, she recalled that kirschwasser was a cherry liqueur. A very expensive liqueur. She grinned at her friend. "I've ordered tiramisu here before, but I never noticed the tastes of almond and cherry liqueur. How in the world do you tell the difference?"

Susannah opened her eyes and reached for another bite. "Breathe out while you're chewing, Kate. That will cause your taste buds to pick up the finer nuances of flavor. Try it."

Closing her eyes, Kate took another small bite, chewed slowly, and exhaled gently at the same time. Her eyes flew open as a burst of flavor seemed to explode in her mouth.

Susannah laughed. "Told you so."

"Amazing," Kate said, then took another bite.

"It's all in how you approach it. Some people eat to sustain life, gobbling down their food to soothe hungry stomachs. Others have discovered the wonderful pleasures to be had in slowing down and savoring each intricate flavor of the foods they eat, whether it be fine chocolate or a cheeseburger with all the fixin's."

Kate widened her eyes. "A cheeseburger?"

"Of course. One of my favorite foods." Susannah chuckled. "But don't tell anyone. It would ruin my reputation." Then her demeanor changed, and she let her gaze drift away from Kate's. "And that's the last thing I need right now," she added.

Kate took a sip of tea, studying her friend.

Susannah looked up and caught her gaze. "This taping is incredibly important," she said. "A lot is riding on it. Yet it seems that someone—or something—is determined to trip me up with my show." She paused, staring into her teacup. "I know you might wonder why I'm telling you this; after all, we haven't been in touch for such a long time. It's not like we're bosom buddies right now." When she looked up, tears glistened in her eyes.

Kate reached for her hand. "We were childhood friends. You practically lived at my house."

Susannah smiled through her tears. "It was your mom who introduced me to the joys one can find in the kitchen. My love affair with chocolate began the Christmas she taught us how to make fudge with marshmallow cream."

Kate smiled at the memory. "We might have been apart all these years, but when I saw you earlier, the years just melted away. We vowed to be best friends for life—do you remember?"

Susannah lifted her teacup, nodded, and took a deep breath. "That has to count for something," she said.

"It counts for a lot," Kate said.

Susannah leaned back in her chair. "The people I'm closest to know nothing of what I'm about to tell you."

Kate's heart went out to her friend. In the blink of an eye, she had gone from bubbly, smiling TV persona to stressed-out businesswoman.

"I'm about to lose everything. My cookbook sales are holding steady—not best sellers by any means, but not tanking either.

"It's my signature bakeware company that has me hanging by a thin thread. After my husband died, I dumped our savings into the start-up, thinking the return would be tenfold, or greater. I thought my name alone would sell the bakeware, but the truth is, I should have put half the money into marketing and advertising. I had advisers, but I didn't listen. I thought I had the Midas touch. Turns out I didn't.

"I have a new cookbook about to come out—*Chocolates to Die For*—and I'm pinning all my hopes on it doing well." She paused. "Actually, to save my bacon, it's got to do better than well. It's got to top the charts."

Kate leaned forward. "So that's why this show is so important. It coincides with the release of your book. Added publicity, better sales."

Susannah suddenly smiled. "You always were a quick study. Yes, that's it exactly."

"You said someone is trying to trip you up."

"Big time."

"In what way?"

"Someone broke into my home office just a few weeks ago. Whoever it was trashed the place. Nothing was missing. No fingerprints. I suspect he—or she—was looking for an advance copy of the manuscript. That would be the only thing of value anyone could possibly want."

Kate studied her friend while the dots connected in her brain. "For the recipes?" she finally said. "To release them as their own before the book is published?"

"You're right again, Katie dear. You always were the smart one."

Kate grinned in spite of herself. "Did they get them—the recipes, I mean?"

Susannah shrugged. "They're on my computer, and someone tried to log on. Unless that person was a total geek and knew how to break into my system without a password, no, I don't think so. But I can't say for sure."

"What about suspects? Can you think of anyone who would want to do this to you?"

Susannah shook her head. "At first I suspected everyone I work with, especially the other chefs. I thought that jealousy might be the motive. It didn't take me long to realize that's no way to live—or to treat your colleagues. Then some other odd occurrences began...." She poured them each another cup of tea, added a lump of sugar to hers, and stirred thoughtfully. "It's sabotage, pure and simple. Things disappear from my soundstage kitchen right before I go on the air. Props turn up missing, and ingredients are substituted—salt for sugar, sugar for salt. If it's only the visuals you care about, that's not a big deal. But this happened in front of a studio audience. The reaction of the guests I'd chosen to taste my creations was terrible. We had to retape the show. Thank goodness it wasn't live."

"And you don't have a clue as to who's doing this?"

She shook her head. "I almost canceled this gig. If it hadn't been for my cookbook, the needed hype, I would have. It also helped to know I had a trusted friend in this town. As soon as you got in touch, that sealed my decision. I knew I had to go through with the show."

Kate looked around. She and Susannah were the only patrons left in the tearoom. The lights were dim in the foyer beyond the open doors. A lone waiter was watching them expectantly. Kate glanced at her watch. It was almost nine, and the tearoom was essentially closed.

"We'd better go," Susannah said, following Kate's gaze. "I didn't realize they were waiting for us to leave."

Kate reached for the bill, but Susannah was quicker. She smiled. "I'll get this one."

The two women walked through the foyer and, for a moment, stood talking at the entryway.

"What can I do to help?" Kate asked.

"I'd love it if you'd keep a close eye on my set before the taping. Tell me if you see any funny business."

"I'd be happy to."

They visited for a few more minutes, then said their good-byes. Kate turned toward the door, then she hesitated and looked back at the retreating Susannah. "Suse," she called out, surprising herself that the childhood nickname came so easily.

"I haven't heard that name in years," Susannah said, looking pleased. "Makes me feel young again."

Kate took a few steps closer. "The question that keeps nagging me is *why*. Why would someone want to sabotage your show, or your cookbook?"

Susannah shrugged. "I've asked myself that dozens of times, and I honestly don't know."

The police had probably asked the same questions, but Kate needed to know the answers too. "Do you have any enemies —anyone you've met over the years who might want to harm you? Someone you went around on your way to the top?"

"Not that I know of."

"How about an adoring fan who's, shall we say, a few eggs short of a carton?"

Susannah groaned and then laughed. "Tasties don't get all that carried away over chefs. But I suppose it's not out of the realm of possibility."

It occurred to Kate that although they had been childhood friends she really didn't know the details of Susannah's life. She seemed like the Susannah of old, but how could Kate know for sure?

She gave her friend a quick good-bye hug and headed through the doorway toward the parking lot. The lot was deserted. Even the Taste Network crew had turned in for the night.

The mist had lifted, but the foliage near the creek still dripped with moisture. As the drops hit wet leaves on the ground, the sound was magnified in the quiet of the night. It almost sounded like footsteps moving along the creek path.

No. It couldn't be. Kate wouldn't allow herself to believe it. But still, she quickened her pace toward the Honda.

She reached her car and started to open her door, then, unable to resist, she pivoted toward the hotel for a last look at the second-floor windows.

Nothing.

With a sigh of relief, she stepped into her car and turned on the ignition. She was just swinging the Honda around toward the parking lot driveway, when a flicker of light caught her eye.

But this time, it wasn't in the hotel windows. It moved along the path to the creek, exactly where she thought she'd heard footsteps.

Her heart caught in her throat. She floored the accelerator and sped out of the parking lot.

Chapter Three

Paul looked up and smiled when Kate came into the kitchen. The heavenly scent of melting chocolate wafted from the pan he was stirring. She slipped off her coat, then gave him a kiss on the cheek before heading to the entryway closet. Paul met her in the living room a few minutes later, two mugs of cocoa in hand.

They sat down in front of the fireplace, and she told him about the strange occurrences at the hotel, her visit with Susannah, the footsteps she'd heard on the path leading to the creek, and the flickering light she'd seen as she was pulling away from the hotel.

"Did you investigate?"

"Do you even need to ask?" She laughed. "I'm going to look at the rooms tomorrow." She grinned. "You know me. Never met a mystery I could leave alone."

He sighed and took a sip of his hot cocoa. "I take it you didn't find anything."

"Actually, no. But it's the strangest thing. I thought I heard footsteps as I was walking to my car. Very light, almost like slippered feet. I could almost have dismissed that as my imagination, but then I saw the flicker of light near the creek." She leaned forward, studying his face. "I've never been one to get too excited about ghosts. In fact, mostly I find the whole idea silly. . . ."

"But?" He quirked a brow.

"You should have seen the . . . well, apparition in the windows, or whatever it was, Paul. It gave me the chills."

"Could it be a hoax?"

"I can't imagine why someone would pull something like that." She watched the flickering flames for a few moments, then took another sip of cocoa, looking at Paul over the rim of her mug.

"Publicity for Joel St. Nicklaus?"

"I wonder about that. Livvy said he's coming to town for a signing." She studied the fire for a moment, then turned again to Paul. "A haunting certainly would guarantee a better turnout for the signing, but he's a well-known investigative reporter. I can't imagine that he would risk his reputation. Besides, these ghost sightings began before the book released."

Paul stood to stoke the fire. A spray of embers crackled and popped.

"I get the impression you're wondering if the ghost is real," he said as he sat down again.

"This is the South. There are a lot of people with solid reputations who've reported seeing ghosts. . . ." She suddenly felt ridiculous and laughed, shaking her head. "Even so, the jury's still out as far as I'm concerned."

Paul squeezed her hand, then said, "And what about Susannah? Was it a good reunion?"

"The best..." She hesitated, remembering her friend's troubled expression. "Let me back up. The reunion was wonderful, but Susannah is facing some tough challenges. I came away from our time together with a heavy heart." She told Paul about the break-in at Susannah's home office and the sabotage attempts on the show set.

They finished their cocoa, and Paul took Kate's hand to help her to her feet. He circled his arm around her waist as they headed to the kitchen and rinsed their mugs. She leaned against him, enveloped in his warmth and smiled as thoughts of ghostly apparitions flitted from her mind.

JUST AS SYBIL PREDICTED, the next morning Kate found nothing unusual in the hotel's upper wing. She spent extra time in the three rooms where the strange flickering lights and ghost-like figure had appeared. The first was obviously used for storage, but not often, Kate surmised, because of the thin layer of dust. It appeared it might have once been used as a conference room. One round table was set up in the center of the room with a half dozen leatherette chairs around it. Several folding banquet tables leaned against one wall.

The second room was used for storing bed linens, pillows, and the such. A couple of mattresses, still plastic wrapped, were propped against one wall. The dust on the floor of both storage rooms was smudged with footprints, though none was distinct. Kate remembered Sybil's investigations after the reported ghost activity and surmised the footprints were hers.

The third room contained cleaning supplies for the housekeepers, vacuum cleaners, mops, buckets, and dozens of spray bottles with generic cleaners.

The laundry room was at the end of the partially carpeted hallway, and after a cursory glance at the industrial washers and dryers and a dumbwaiter that appeared to lead downstairs, Kate moved on to the opposite side of the hallway and the four rooms that faced away from the parking lot.

Nothing struck her as being out of the ordinary. Three rooms were made up as if waiting for guests, though they smelled musty. The lock on the fourth door wouldn't open with the master key card Sybil had loaned her. She made a note to check with Sybil later about that room, which was directly across from the laundry room.

She was surprised at the location of the laundry room. If she had designed the hotel, she would have put it downstairs to save the housekeeping staff the extra footwork. At least the dumbwaiter in the corner sent up the dirty laundry so the workers didn't have to carry it upstairs.

As she headed back downstairs to Sybil's office, she thought about the activities going on in what she was beginning to think of as the "ghost wing" of the hotel. During the day, the maids and service people were likely to be buzzing in and out, so there was very little chance for ghost activity during those hours. But at night when no one was around . . .

A moment later, Kate rapped on Sybil's door, then opened it as soon as she was invited in.

Sybil looked up and smiled as Kate approached her desk. She looked much more composed than she'd been the night before.

"Did you find anything?" Her expression said she knew the answer.

Kate shook her head. "But I do have a couple of questions."

"Shoot."

She handed Sybil the master key card. "This worked in every lock except the last room on the right-hand side—room 213. Were you aware of that?"

Sybil frowned, then shook her head. "I'm surprised. It's always worked for me."

But Kate saw something behind Sybil's eyes that said she wasn't telling the whole truth.

A moment of silence fell between them, but Kate didn't press. "Something else I wondered," she said. "The guests who've reported seeing things—unusual things, shall we say?—have those occurrences been in the daytime or at night?"

"Mostly at night," Sybil said. "Why?"

"Just trying to connect some dots," Kate said. She hesitated, then added, "By the way, is there a blueprint of the hotel around someplace that I could have a look at?"

"A blueprint?"

"Or a map—maybe you have a drawing of the hotel layout you give guests so they can find their way around. Something like that."

"Oh yes. Of course." She opened a file drawer and handed Kate a brochure-like drawing of the hotel. Kate gave it a glance, nodded when she found what she was looking for, then smiled her thanks and turned to leave.

"Kate?"

She turned back to Sybil, noting the dark circles beneath her eyes and her gaunt cheeks.

"There is something else I should tell you—"

Just then, a loud crash, followed by shouting, reverberated down the hallway from the foyer.

Sybil shot up from her desk like a rocket. Kate stepped out of her way as she swished by, then followed her toward the foyer. Kate was only a half pace behind her.

There, on the floor in front of the reception desk, lay a large boom mike. To Kate, it resembled a toppled metal giraffe. A young, red-haired crew member stood nearby, white-faced, while Newt Keller berated him. A hush had fallen over the foyer.

The young man finally found his tongue and interrupted the tirade. "S-sir, it was an accid—" His face flushed almost the color of his hair.

Newt raised his hand, palm out, to stop him. "Do you have any idea the cost involved in something like this?" His tone was belittling, sarcastic. "Not just the money but the time to find a replacement for the boom and, I might add, for you?"

Kate's hackles were standing on end, and she felt her own face go warm on behalf of the young man.

From the back of the crowd, a voice called Newt's name. It was authoritative, no nonsense, and completely in control. Kate would have known the voice anywhere. She watched as Susannah made her way to the boom. She stood directly in front of Newt and glared at him, hands on her hips.

"You have no right to speak to Jack this way, Newt," she said, quietly, calmly.

The producer stepped back almost as if he'd been slapped. "Who do you think you are? You have no right to interfere," he growled.

"And you, dear sir"—she stepped closer and tapped his chest with her forefinger to emphasize each word—"have no right to berate any of the Taste Network employees ... make that any human being ... in such a manner. Someday you'll be sorry."

"Is that a threat, Susannah?"

She didn't answer. Instead, she glanced at the young man, who looked like he was finally able to breathe again. He swept his fingers through his red hair and gave her a shaky smile.

"These are my people, my employees," Newt said, "which means I have the power to hire, fire, and call them up short when they need it."

"Okay, Mr. Bigshot," said a voice behind Kate. She turned as Birdie Birge stepped forward with a confident smile. "Now that you've attempted to put us all in our places, don't you think it's time we got to work?"

Behind Birdie stood Nicolette Pascal, who remained silent. Before the pretty, dark-haired woman turned away, Kate thought she saw a hint of a smirk. But Nicolette wasn't leering at Newt Keller; her gaze was fixed on Susannah.

Chapter Four

I'll be the one who determines our work schedule," Newt Keller said, still huffing.

But Kate could see the tension had broken. She wondered how often the chefs and crew had to stand up for one another against his tirades. Already, she had noticed a pattern. Newt kept everyone off balance with his mood swings—easy-going comrade one minute, harsh taskmaster the next. She couldn't imagine the tension of working under such conditions. She breathed a prayer for his employees.

Ten minutes later, Kate headed up the risers of the makeshift studio-audience space. A few of those who had come out to welcome the cast and crew the night before were there: Eli Weston shot Kate a wide smile and waved. Willy Bergen, sitting next to him, did the same. Sam Gorman, who had tromped up the risers just before Kate, sat on a chair next to Willy. Joe Tucker followed and plumped down on Sam's opposite side. Many of the businesses in town were closed for a couple of hours, so everyone in Copper Mill would be able to enjoy what they could of the tapings.

LuAnne Matthews, Millie Lovelace, and Livvy Jenner

had already taken their places a couple of rows down from the rest of the group. Livvy sat at the end of the row with an extra space beside her. As Kate made her way toward her friend, Renee called "*Yoo-hoo!*" from the bottom row.

When Kate turned, Renee said, "Save us a place!" It was a demand, not a request. "I have something important to tell you."

Kate breathed a little prayer for grace and nodded that she would.

Trailing behind Renee was Kisses, on his jeweled leash, and Caroline, with a flashy, apparently new jeweled cane.

Everyone scooted down to make room as the mother-daughter-Chihuahua team moved into the row, a cloud of Estée Lauder's Youth-Dew, Renee's signature scent, descending upon all.

Renee, who was now sitting to Kate's left, leaned toward her conspiratorially, her hand covering her mouth. "You won't believe what I've heard."

Kate sighed. She didn't like gossip and tried her best to avoid it, but sometimes she felt trapped . . . usually by Renee.

She held up a hand. "If it's gos—"

"Oh goodness, no. I don't do gossip," Renee said. "No, this has to do with what's going on at Faith Briar."

Which meant it was probably gossip.

Just then, activity at the front of the set caught their attention. A bouncy young woman Kate hadn't seen before hurried across the room and onto the soundstage.

The woman looked up at the audience members seated in folding chairs on the risers and gave them a wide grin.

"Hi, everybody!" she called out. Her tone reminded Kate of a cheerleader at a pep rally.

The woman was dark-haired, petite, and high-energy. Her face looked vaguely familiar, but Kate couldn't place her.

"My name is Daryl Gallagher," she said. "I'm the assistant producer and director of the shows we'll be taping this week." She paused with a cute shrug, then continued. "Actually, that's a pretty long important-sounding title for what I really do. I'm actually what's called a GGF." She raised a brow as if waiting for a sign that the audience knew what she was talking about. Then she laughed. "That's Go-fer Girl Friday. But don't you go calling me Gopher Girl." She laughed again.

The audience laughed with her.

"Whoa . . . you're good," she said. "That's what we want to hear. Laughter. Cheers. Sighs of ecstasy when something gorgeous comes out of the oven. And above all, we want you to look like you're absolutely dying for a bite of whatever it is. Don't drool, but look like you're about to. The camera will be panning the audience, so your friends and relatives may even see your smiling faces on TV." Daryl laughed again, glanced back at the studio kitchen behind her, and walked toward it as she continued her pep talk.

Kate was astounded at how the hotel had accommodated the network, letting them take over a conference room that backed up to the kitchen of the Bristol. The resulting studio kitchen looked as if it was part of the hotel, not brought in by truck the night before.

The kitchen was raised onto a platform about a foot off the main floor. On the platform were two large built-in refrigerators, two restaurant-sized ovens, and an island stovetop and

sink combination—all set in cabinets that appeared to be custom made, straight out of House Beautiful. The floor had been
laid with travertine tile, which picked up the color of the
Tuscan-style cabinets. Utensils were in place, ingredients
already measured out on the counter for the first taping, with
measuring cups and spoons nearby, pots and pans within arm's
reach, and pot holders strategically placed.

The entire set looked warm and inviting, especially the four
round bistro tables right in front of the soundstage. Behind the
kitchen set, but hidden from view, was the Bristol's kitchen.
On the opposite side, an open doorway led to the hotel foyer.

"As I was saying," Renee whispered to Kate. "I've got news
about the ghost sightings. . . ."

"What does that have to do with Faith Briar?"

Renee gave Kate a look that said she wondered if Kate
had just arrived from Mars.

"People want to know if ghosts are real. If they can't get
through to Paul, they call me. I had three phone calls after I
got home last night—all from members of Faith Briar." She
lifted her chin a notch. "Naturally, since I'm a member of the
church board, they're interested in my opinion." She arched
a brow and sniffed importantly.

"Oh, hush now," Caroline said to her daughter. "Can't you
see this little cheerleader gal is about to get the ball rolling?"

Daryl bounded onto the soundstage and turned toward
the audience. "We'll do a run-through or two when the chef
arrives. Susannah Applebaum is first up today." She glanced
at her watch with an irritated expression. "She should have
been here by now. She always likes to say a few words to the
audience before we begin."

A lanky young man appeared from somewhere behind the set. He moved toward Daryl as if entranced by her vivacious beauty. Before reaching her, he tripped over a potted plant someone had placed at the edge of the set. He caught himself, grinned, then looked out at the audience.

"Hi, all," he said with a half wave. He looked back at Daryl. "I'm sorry. I didn't mean to interrupt." He flushed. "Susannah Applebaum told me I ought to drop in and introduce myself," he said, regaining his composure. "I'm Armand Platt." He doffed his chef's hat and gave her an exaggerated bow.

"Yes, I know," Daryl said. "The new intern here at the Bristol." Her tone said she wasn't impressed. "Straight out of culinary arts school, right?"

Armand didn't seem offended by the dig. Instead, he flashed a good-natured smile. "That's right. And Susannah said to tell you that if you need someone to fill in at any time, I'm your man."

He grabbed a couple of wooden spoons from the counter and did a drumroll. Kate thought she saw his ears waggle. The audience laughed.

Then a chill fell over the room as a scowling Newt Keller strode in holding a clipboard.

"Where is everybody?" he demanded, glaring at Daryl.

"Everybody?" she said, frowning. "As in . . ."

"You know who I'm talking about. Ms. Prima Donna herself." He laughed as if the sarcastic remark was a joke. No one laughed with him.

"Prima donna? *Moi?*" Susannah stepped out from behind the set. She was drying her hands on a tea towel, which she threw over her shoulder Emeril Lagasse-style. She'd obviously been working on something in the Bristol's kitchen with Armand and had probably heard every word Newt said.

"I resent the implication, Newt. I think an apology is in order, not just to me, but to all the people you've stepped on in the past twenty-four hours." She gave an exaggerated wink, obviously trying to keep the tone light for the audience's sake. But the tension between them was thick.

He laughed. "You have to be kidding."

"I'm not kidding at all," she said, still grinning. Then she looked out at the audience and winked again before turning back to Newt. "Apologies can be terribly good for the soul. You might want to try one sometime."

A spontaneous cheer rose from both the crew and the audience. Susannah beamed and bowed with a flourish. "See, I told you so," she said to the producer. "They'll love you for it."

Newt stared at her for a heartbeat, then with a glare that took in stagehands, makeup artists, hair and wardrobe people, and the camera crew, he said, "All right, everybody, let's get back to work."

Susannah smiled sweetly. "I agree."

"Whoa," Caroline sang out from down the row. "For a minute, I thought there was going to be trouble right here in River City. Trouble with a capital *T* and that rhymes with—"

"Mama, we don't need to hear you sing from *The Music Man*," Renee said, then added under her breath, "'Seventy-six Trombones' will be next."

"You can say that again," LuAnne said. "I mean, the trouble with a capital *T* part. I feel it in my bones." Murmurs of agreement rose from those who were sitting nearby.

Kate didn't comment, but an ominous cloud settled over her. Trouble was lurking around the corner, and it wasn't just because of a ghost.

Chapter Five

Renee elbowed Kate's arm. "Look at this, will you?" She held out her cell phone and pointed to the screen. "I told you about those calls. Three more have come in since we sat down." She tapped her phone. "I recognize the numbers— they're all from Faith Briar members." An eyebrow shot up. "Just like I told you."

"Who wants your opinion?" Caroline said.

"That's privileged information."

"But I'm your mother."

"You don't even go to our church."

"Well, the folks at St. Lucy's are as concerned as those at Faith Briar," Caroline said. "You wouldn't believe how they're taking sides. Some have quit speaking to each other. My friends call those who say they believe in ghosts Caspers."

"Caspers?" Kate almost choked. "Really?" She glanced at Livvy, who was grinning.

"Appropriate, if you ask me," Livvy said.

"Hush now, everyone," Renee said. "It looks like they're about ready to start."

Kate turned her attention back to the set. Newt Keller had fixed his sights on Daryl Gallagher. "So why are you just standing there? Let's get the crew out here and do our run-through. Where are they, anyway?" The man surely had a split personality, Kate thought, one minute flashing a smile that would charm an angel, the next, spewing rude demands that could devastate the toughest of souls.

Caroline said in a loud whisper, "That boy's mama didn't teach him any manners. If he'd been a child of mine, I would have set him straight."

Joe Tucker broke the tension with another Groucho imitation. "I'd hoped that little French chef would be here today. I'm looking forward to seeing her sashay around the kitchen."

"Sashay, my foot," Caroline muttered.

The young woman in the black smock was still standing in front of Susannah with an open suitcase full of makeup. She applied gloss to Susannah's lips, then stood back to admire her work while a twenty-something man with a bleached spiky do teased, sprayed, and arranged Susannah's chin-length blonde bob.

Susannah didn't seem to even notice. Instead, she used the time to go over her script while the crew took care of the last-minute details on the set, testing the sound system, the camera angle, and lighting.

After the makeup artist left the stage with her rollaway suitcase full of powders and paints, Susannah glanced toward the back of the kitchen set as if looking for someone. She spotted Armand Platt standing off to one side, chef's hat still in one hand, and gestured to him.

Armand glanced around to see if she was focused on

someone behind him. Susannah laughed and beckoned to him to come over.

Kate couldn't hear what was said, but Armand beamed and nodded vigorously.

Ten minutes later, it was obvious what the conversation had been about. When the run-through began, Armand was in the studio kitchen with Susannah, trying to remember where to stand and what to do. He bungled the first rehearsal so badly they had to start over again. Kate was amazed at Susannah's patience.

During the second rehearsal, Armand fumbled a saucepan filled with melted chocolate, but both the crew and the studio audience applauded and cheered when he caught it without spilling a drop. He grinned and bowed with a flourish, doffing his chef's hat once more. Kate thought the moment was priceless.

It was obvious Newt Keller didn't agree.

The producer-director sat in his chair off to one side of the stage, his face rocket red, making Kate wonder about his blood pressure.

After a brief conversation with Daryl, he settled back and watched as Daryl gave Armand additional instructions about where to stand. One of the crew members hovered nearby, drawing chalk Xs on the travertine tile to help Armand remember.

"They're giving the boy one last chance," Renee whispered.

Kate nodded.

After another brief break and audience pep talk from Daryl, the show was ready to tape.

A hush fell over the studio. Daryl did the countdown, then pointed to camera one. The red light went on.

Susannah made her grand entrance, bowing and blowing kisses to the audience. She was dressed in her chef's jacket over black slacks, looking every bit the part of a celebrity chef. Her smile and laugh were contagious as she bantered with the audience, then positioned herself in front of the camera, which was between the kitchen and the studio audience.

Camera two rolled noiselessly along an elevated track, above the kitchen.

"Today I'm going to start with one of my favorite recipes from my new cookbook, *Chocolates to Die For*. It's a surprising combination of ingredients that will not only meld in taste; they'll also melt in your mouth. You might think hot cocoa is good only for drinking around a campfire with s'mores, or for giving to the kids on a wintery day, but I think you'll change your mind once you taste my sumptuous to-die-for *chocolaté dos mundos*."

She bounded into the kitchen, smiling and twirling, mugging to the camera, and chatting at the studio audience as if she were best friends with each person sitting in front of her.

With Armand at her side, she measured the ingredients, explaining as she proceeded. "In Mexico there's a saying, 'In order for a cup of chocolate to be perfect, it must be hot, sweet, thick, and made by the hands of a woman.'" She grinned at Armand. "Sorry, bud, but that's the saying."

He saluted her. "I am but your student. What your hands teach, mine will attempt," he said smiling.

Susannah turned again to the camera. "This luscious drink features whole milk, half-and-half, chocolate, cinnamon, Mexican vanilla, almond extract, and"—she looked up at Armand again—"drumroll, please."

He grabbed a couple of wooden spoons and did his second drum solo of the morning with an even greater flourish. He finished with a cymbal-like crash of two saucepan lids. The audience loved it.

Susannah laughed. "I believe we've got a new Taste Network star in the making." The studio audience clapped and cheered as Armand bowed.

"But don't forget to stir the chocolate while you're hamming it up." She placed another wooden spoon in his hand and pointed him toward the stove.

"Now, back to the ingredients," she said, picking up a small metal tin. "To give my chocolate drink an extra kick, we're going to add a generous pinch of ancho and chipotle chilies."

On a cue from Daryl, the audience gasped.

Beside Kate, Renee groaned and Caroline whispered, "She just ruined the whole thing."

Susannah moved from the chocolate drink to Belgian chocolate bars, made with white chocolate, orange oil, crystallized dates, and walnuts.

"Each bar has layers of taste and texture," she said. "What I call the surprise of chocolate."

As the studio audience nibbled on samples, the camera panned the room.

After a short break during which Susannah's nose was powdered and lip gloss reapplied, she came over toward the studio audience. She blew kisses to Kate, waved to a few others she'd met, then stepped back onto the stage.

"Remember, fellow Tasties, chocolate in its purity is a beautiful thing. That's about it for now. From all of us at *Sumptuous Chocolates*, good-bye and God bless." She blew kisses at the camera, then said with a wink, "Until we eat again . . ."

The studio audience stood and cheered. A flushed and obviously pleased Susannah grinned at them, then invited all to come up and enjoy a sample of the rich chocolate drink.

"Not so fast," Newt roared. "We need to do this again."

Susannah whirled toward him. "What do you mean, do this again? It may have some rough spots, but they can be edited out. It was a great show."

"The humor was stilted," he said, striding toward the stage. "Felt forced. The TV audience will pick up on it like that." He snapped his fingers, then moved his piercing stare to Armand, who was leaning against one of the refrigerators, an ankle hooked over the opposite foot.

Newt pointed at the young intern. "He has no business horning his way onto Taste Network like this. You should have seen through his antics. He was just looking for a way to get his foot in the door. Probably wants a show of his own. And you fell for it. Worse, you encouraged it." He stepped onto the stage, glaring at her.

A hush had fallen over the studio. Kate was almost afraid to breathe, wondering what was coming next. She didn't have to wait long.

Susannah stared at Newt for a moment without speaking. Then something seemed to snap inside her. "You—" she said, closing the remaining distance between them with measured steps. "You have just said your last nasty words to me. I will not take this any longer. Your treatment of others is abusive and not to be tolerated."

"Are you threatening me again?" Newt sneered.

By now Armand—no longer looking jovial—had moved away from the refrigerator. He walked over to Newt and shoved him.

"If you don't take it as a threat from Miss Applebaum, you can take it as a threat from me. Don't ever speak to her or anyone else in my presence with that tone. And don't ever accuse me of trying to horn in on your network again. I wouldn't work for you if my life depended on it."

Newt gave him a sarcastic smile. "A threat, you said. Tell me what that threat would be."

For a heartbeat, Armand just stared at the producer. "You don't want to know," he said. Then he took off his chef's jacket and hat, threw them down, and stomped from the studio.

Susannah slumped against one of the kitchen counters, shaking her head slowly. "You know how much we love working for Taste, Newt. We want the network to succeed as much as you do. But you're going to lose all of us if you continue to belittle us," she said quietly. "I've warned you already. Here's another to add to the growing list: If you speak to any of us again with disrespect, you'll be sorry. You seem to forget that keeping us happy improves the ratings—and isn't that what it's all about? Ratings?"

"I'm the one who knows what works and what doesn't for our audiences," Newt said. "I'm the one who studies the demographics, who knows all the nuances of everything from overall programming to individual show content." He took a step closer to Susannah. The cherubic smile had returned, but his eyes looked hard, even from where Kate was sitting.

"Since you've given me a threat, let me give you one," he said. "There are at least a dozen top-notch chefs waiting to be part of Taste Network. If you don't like the way I operate, you can simply go back to where you came from. One phone call, and I can fill your spot."

"Yet another instance of your lack of respect for us," Susannah said. "I'd hoped for better."

"Hear, hear," called out another voice. From behind the set, Birdie Birge suddenly appeared, looking madder than a wet Rhode Island Red. "That goes double for me—and probably everyone else within earshot. We're gonna start taking numbers, next thing you know."

Stiff-shouldered, she turned and followed Susannah through the doorway leading to the hotel foyer.

Kate let out a pent-up breath, grabbed her handbag, and hurried after them. She spotted both women at the bottom of one of the large twin staircases leading to the second floor.

"Susannah," she called. "Wait."

Susannah and Birdie turned. As Kate drew closer, she could see the tremor in her friend's movement, the pallor of her skin.

Kate gave her a hug. "Hey, are you all right?"

Susannah shook her head. "I'm ready to walk if he pulls this again."

"You and me both," Birdie sniffed.

Kate glanced across the foyer toward the tearoom. "How about a cup of tea?"

Susannah sighed deeply. "A good cup of tea does wonders for the spirit."

"Amen to that," Birdie said. She gave the tearoom a longing gaze. "In fact, next to a big bowl of grits, I can't think of anything I'd like better."

"Unless it would be to get rid of our producer," Susannah said.

Birdie laughed. "Like that could ever happen."

Chapter Six

The women had just ordered a plateful of finger sandwiches when Kate heard the Taste crew and audience members vacating the studio and moving into the adjoining foyer.

"That's about the only thing Newt does right," Susannah said. "He gives generous lunch breaks—usually a couple of hours."

Birdie snorted. "Only because he wants to get away from the studio himself. Self-serving motives."

A handful of network crew members drifted into the tearoom, but most headed for the hotel exit, probably to have lunch at the diner.

Kate looked up as the third member of the celebrity-chef trio, Nicolette Pascal, came through the door with Daryl Gallagher. The resemblance, once she saw the two of them together, was striking.

Susannah noticed Kate's startled expression. "Mother and daughter."

"I was going to guess sisters," Kate said in surprise.

Birdie chuckled. "Let's just say that one of the two keeps herself looking very young . . . and keeps a Beverly Hills plastic surgeon very happy. I'll leave it to you to guess which one."

Though she didn't know Nicolette or Daryl, Kate didn't care for the dig or the gossip. Judging from Susannah's expression, her friend didn't either.

The two women stopped by the table just as the waiter brought the tiered crystal plate of finger sandwiches.

Nicolette's smile was tight as she surveyed the three women, and Kate suspected it wasn't caused by her numerous face-lifts. Her gaze beaded in on Susannah. "I hear things didn't go well this morning." Her voice held the hint of a French accent.

"I thought the show went very well," Susannah said, flushing. "Though I admit there was disagreement in the studio."

"You can say that again," Daryl said sympathetically.

"Constructive criticism can be a difficult pill to swallow," Nicolette said, "even if it's given for our benefit."

"I agreed with Susannah this time, Mother," Daryl said. "Newt was completely out of line."

Nicolette tilted her head. "Really," she said with a half smile. Then she added, strangely, "You have beautiful skin, Susannah."

Susannah frowned. "I do?"

Nicolette nodded. "You'll probably never have to have any work done, if you know what I mean."

"Well, thank you," Susannah said.

"When a person is overweight, they can be assured their wrinkles will be minimal. It's especially nice in front of the camera."

"Mother!" Daryl looked stunned.

Kate caught her breath at the dig. Susannah turned bright red, and Birdie gaped.

"What did you say?" Birdie's disbelief was evident in her

tone. "I can't believe what I just heard, especially considering I'm the one who—"

Looking embarrassed by her mother's words, Daryl held up a hand. "Ladies, I think my mother and I need to be seated. The hostess is glaring at us from her station." Then she added, her gaze on Susannah, "If you'll excuse us . . ." And the mother-daughter duo walked across the room to their own table.

"Somebody needs to," Birdie muttered once they were out of earshot. Then she reached across the table and patted Susannah's hand. "Don't let her rude remarks disturb you. She's just envious of your ratings. It's her feeble attempt to bring you down a notch."

"I'm not disturbed," Susannah said. "I like myself the way I am." She picked up her teacup and took a sip, studying the other two women above the rim of her cup. She placed it back in the saucer and sighed. "But I do have to admit this conflict is getting to me. I'm beginning to think maybe this place really *is* haunted. I don't discount Newt Keller's rudeness, but on the other hand, I've never seen such nettlesome behavior among the cast and crew. It's as if there are gremlins running around here trying to tie us all in knots."

"Gremlins?" Birdie laughed. "The only gremlin around here is Newt. And he's more of an ogre than a gremlin. Talk about the one who's nettlesome, peevish, testy . . . Shall I go on?"

Susannah chuckled. "I think we get the picture."

The women finished their tea and sandwiches, said their good-byes, then went their separate ways for the remainder of the lunch break—Susannah to her room to prepare for the afternoon taping, and Birdie to hers to rest.

Kate drove home to fix lunch for Paul, only to find that

he'd left a note saying he was having lunch at the diner with the other pastors in town to discuss the issue of ghosts.

Kate wasn't hungry, but she felt the need to mull things over, so she pulled out her mixer and the ingredients for her cranberry-walnut oatmeal cookies. There was nothing like baking to help connect the dots in a mystery. She was especially inspired after being around the network that morning.

She turned on the mixer to cream the eggs and butter, frowning as she worked.

Two mysteries were bothering her: First, the strange hauntings at the Hamilton Springs. Second, the reported mischief in Susannah's studio kitchen.

She added the sifted flour and turned on the mixer again. Her thoughts shifted from the Hamilton Springs ghost to, in her opinion, the more critical of the two mysteries: the sabotaging of her friend's studio kitchen—and possibly her career.

Who would do such a thing? And why?

She ran through the list of possibilities . . . but none of the suspects or motives seemed plausible.

After she finished adding the dry ingredients, she turned off the mixer. She poured in her secret ingredient—a capful of almond extract—then stirred in the dried cranberries and nuts.

A quick glance at the clock told her she had just enough time to bake one sheet of cookies for Paul. She spooned the dough onto the sheet, placed it in the oven, and set the timer.

Still pondering her very short list of suspects, Kate sighed and sat down at her oak dining table. Who stood to gain the most from the failure of *Sumptuous Chocolates*?

One of the other chefs? If so, Nicolette Pascal and

Birdie Birge were top suspects, at least until she could prove otherwise.

Kate rubbed her forehead. She loved it when cookie baking brought a breakthrough in her mystery mullings. Unfortunately, she wasn't having one of those days.

Another idea hit her at the same moment the timer chimed. She pulled the cookie sheet out of the oven, turned off the heat, then trotted to Paul's office and sat down in front of the computer. They didn't have a high-speed Internet connection, so any research she did at home seemed to take forever. She preferred the computers at the library, which surfed the Web at lightning speed, as well as the company of her dear friend Livvy. But she was in a time crunch, and using a sluggish computer beat taking a detour to the library.

She did a search for "Susannah Applebaum," clicked on the first site, then sat back and waited . . . and waited . . . and waited as it loaded. Finally, the site was up. Susannah's photograph was in the right-hand corner, with an article beneath it. Kate's heart sank as she read.

FIFTEEN MINUTES LATER, Kate settled into her seat in the studio audience. Renee and Caroline and all the others were in their same seats.

"Guess what we did," Caroline said to Kate.

Kate turned in her seat. "I can't imagine . . ."

"Eli drove a bunch of us down to the Mercantile to buy the ingredients for the chocolate drink."

Renee broke in. "Well, we bought what ingredients they had. It seems nobody's ever asked for Mexican vanilla or powder of ancho and chipotle chilies before."

LuAnne laughed. "You could've knocked the clerk over with a feather when we told him it was for hot cocoa."

Renee sniffed. "A drink like that isn't called cocoa."

"If it's not cocoa, I'll eat my hat," Joe Tucker said, his voice booming from two rows back.

"Get out the ketchup, then," Renee sniffed. "Because Susannah herself called it *Chocolaté Dos Mundos*. She also referred to it as the champagne of all chocolate drinks. Never once did she call it cocoa."

Kisses, who was sitting on Renee's lap, seemed agitated. He growled and kept his eyes on the doorway leading to the foyer.

"There, there, Little Umpkins," Renee soothed. "Settle down."

But Kisses wouldn't settle.

"You know," Renee said, "about this ghost business . . . it's said that animals have a sense of that kind of activity. Have you ever observed a cat watching something in the air that you can't see?"

Millie Lovelace overheard the conversation and leaned forward. "It's true. I've seen it firsthand."

"There've been other times," Renee said, "when I swear Little Umpkins sees things I can't. It happens all the time at home, doesn't it, Mama?"

Caroline harrumphed. "He's just watching a gnat do loopdeloops. There's nothing ghostly about that."

Kate checked her watch and frowned. The taping was supposed to start at two o'clock sharp. It was now a quarter past, and there was no sign of Susannah. Or Newt Keller.

No one onstage seemed too concerned. Daryl was her spirited self, chatting with audience members and crew as they set up for the shoot.

Kate kept an eye out for anything unusual with the setup in the kitchen. Jack, the red-haired kid who dropped the boom mike earlier that day, had apparently been demoted from sound-man to kitchen assistant. He joked with others in the crew as he placed the ingredients in bowls and set them on the counter. Utensils and saucepans from the morning segment had been washed and put away, and the kitchen looked spotless.

Kate breathed a quick prayer for Susannah, hoping the afternoon taping would go much smoother than the morning session. When Kate had driven into the parking lot almost half an hour earlier, she'd noticed that Susannah's little silver Miata was missing. At lunch, her friend had said she was going upstairs to rest.

Where could she have gone?

Kate checked her watch again: 2:31.

Daryl paced in front of the soundstage, giving crew members directions, checking her watch, rearranging dishes and utensils, then checking her watch again. She was still all smiles, but Kate could almost feel the young woman's agitation.

At a quarter to three, Daryl called across the stage to Jack. "I need someone to go up to Newt's room and let him know we're waiting. Would you mind?"

Jack turned red and swallowed hard. "Me?"

"Yes, you. Please. And on your way up, check on Susannah. She usually runs late, but not this late."

Jack flew through the door less than ten minutes later. "He's not there. Neither is she ... Miss Applebaum, I mean. They're both gone. I checked the parking lot. His Hummer's missing. So's her Miata."

Chapter Seven

"It was the strangest thing," Kate said to Paul at dinner that night. She took a bite of his award-winning chili and closed her eyes, savoring the tastes slowly as she exhaled, just as Susannah had told her to do.

"Is something wrong?"

She opened her eyes and laughed. "Oh goodness, no. I'm just practicing becoming a foodie, savoring every hint of flavor."

He took a bite, chomping with relish. No slow savoring for her man. She loved him for it.

"You were saying . . ." he prompted.

"That Susannah and Newt Keller both disappeared."

"Could they have been together?"

"Not likely. He has a bright yellow Hummer. And she drives a little silver Miata. Both vehicles were gone from the parking lot."

"It sounds like the morning was pretty rough sailing. Maybe they each chose to get away and clear their heads."

"That's my feeling as well, but still, I can't get over some of the threats the cast and crew made to Keller." She sighed. "The man has a lot of enemies."

Paul frowned. "Aren't you jumping to conclusions?"

She smiled. "Borrowing trouble, as my mother used to say. You may be right; it seems that way ..."

"Why am I sensing a 'but' about to make an appearance?"

"You know me well. I did an Internet search this afternoon —typed in Susannah's name just to see what might come up."

"And?"

"According to the article I read, there's a lawsuit about to be filed against her. Someone got an advance copy of her book *Chocolates to Die For* and has accused her of plagiarism. Not formally, but the accuser put the charge out there for the public to see."

Paul put down the piece of corn bread he was about to butter. "That's not good news. Do you think the source is reliable?"

"It wasn't a blog. It was in the opinion section of an industry newsletter, *Chef's Corner International*. And you won't believe this: The writer said his source was someone within the Taste Network. But Susannah's a master chocolatier. She's even been inducted into the Chocolate Hall of Fame. I really don't think she would stoop to copying someone else's recipes."

"Plagiarism's a pretty serious charge. Does it mean there will be a lawsuit?"

"Nothing was said about formal charges." Kate took another bite of chili. "It's clear to me that someone doesn't want that cookbook published. Why, I don't know. Somehow it fits into the same category as the break-in at her home office and the studio-kitchen tampering."

Paul shot her a smile as he stood to clear their dishes from the table. "I'm hoping this means more cookies are on the way while you puzzle out this latest wrinkle. The ones you made this afternoon were the best yet." He grabbed a plate of cranberry-walnut oatmeal cookies and brought it to the table.

Kate chuckled. "Wait till I serve you *Chocolaté Dos Mundos.* Talk about chocolate to die for ..."

THE NEXT MORNING, Kate arrived at the hotel a few minutes before eight. The parking lot was full, though she suspected that most of the cars belonged to the studio audience rather than the hotel guests. Which brought her back to Sybil's dispute with Newt Keller over capitalizing on the notoriety of the hotel as a premier site for ghost watching.

Now *that* she could believe of the man. It didn't surprise her that he wasn't sympathetic to the hotel's plight.

She reached the hotel entrance and turned, realizing she hadn't seen Keller's bright yellow Hummer. She scanned the packed parking lot. That vehicle would stand out from the crowd.

It wasn't there.

But Susannah's Miata was. Kate let out a sigh of relief. Then she squinted as something caught her eye: caked, dried mud on the tires and wheel wells.

Curious, she walked closer to the car and stooped down to get a better look. It was a kind of red clay she'd seen somewhere before. She pondered it for a moment but couldn't remember where.

The door to the Sumptuous Chocolates coach whooshed open, startling Kate. She stood so fast she almost lost her balance.

All smiles, Susannah descended the steps, dressed just as she had been the day before—black slacks and a gleaming white chef's jacket.

"What a pleasant surprise to find you at my doorstep." She walked over to where Kate stood by the Miata. Then she frowned as she followed Kate's gaze to the muddy tires. "You're probably wondering where I disappeared to yesterday afternoon."

"Not just me. The audience, the crew ... Everyone was worried." She fell in step with Susannah as the two headed for the hotel entrance.

"And I can only imagine what Newt had to say about the no-show."

There was something in Susannah's expression that bothered Kate, but she couldn't pin it down.

"He wasn't here either."

Susannah stopped in her tracks. "You're kidding. Mr. Perfect actually missed a taping?" She chuckled. "I wish I'd known. I would have enjoyed my afternoon a lot more." Again, the fleeting, indiscernible look.

They reached the entrance, and Kate opened the door to let her friend enter the foyer.

"He'll probably still give me grief this morning. If not for missing the taping yesterday, he'll conjure up something else." She shook her head slowly, then stopped next to the entrance leading to the studio kitchen and risers. "Kate, there's more going on in my life that I haven't told you about. For one of the first times in my life, I'm feeling completely bumfuzzled."

"Bumfuzzled?"

Susannah grinned. "My word for overwhelmed. I don't feel quite so overwhelmed if I call it by a different name." Her expression sobered. "I can't tell you everything right now, but I promise I will as soon as I can. Seriously, Kate, I need your prayers."

"You have them, Suse."

"I remember how your family prayed together when we were kids. And I can see a peace and calm in you that I envy. Something tells me you spend a lot of time in prayer."

Kate started to say something, but Susannah held up a hand to continue. "All I'm saying is that someday maybe I'll be able to pray again, but in the meantime, will you pray for me? I've never needed it more."

Kate gave her a hug. "You didn't even need to ask."

Susannah smiled, then regaining her composure, hurried off toward Daryl, presumably to discuss the taping, and Kate headed up the risers to where her friends were already seated.

Livvy adjusted her chair to make room for Kate to sit down. Renee moved hers slightly in the opposite direction, though Kisses, who'd been sitting in Kate's seat, didn't budge. A puff of Youth-Dew descended on them all as Renee stood to retrieve Kisses from his perch. He cast a doleful look at Kate as if she'd caused him personal injury by requiring him to move.

Kate settled in. Caroline leaned toward her. "That Newt Keller character still isn't here."

"Maybe he went out to breakfast," LuAnne said. "Sometimes service at the diner can be slow, especially when I'm not around to set things in order," she said with a wink.

"Maybe Newt never came back," Millie Lovelace said. "After lunch yesterday, I mean."

"Maybe somebody did him in," Caroline muttered under her breath.

"Mama, that's a terrible thing to say," Renee sniffed, giving her mother a sharp look.

"You heard it here first," Caroline said.

Daryl Gallagher strode to the front of the studio audience and asked for everyone's attention. "Thank you all for coming, and I'm delighted to announce that I will be directing this morning's segment as a guest fill-in for Newt Keller."

Kate leaned forward, her heart thumping out a staccato beat. Trouble here in River City indeed.

"I told you so," Caroline whispered.

Several people in front of Kate exchanged worried glances. Strangely, the onstage crew members seemed to take the news in stride, going about their work as if their producer's disappearance was expected.

Or maybe they were just relieved.

The makeup artist had set up her portable makeup table and lighted mirror to one side of the soundstage. Susannah seemed much more relaxed as she sat down in front of the mirror. The artist picked up a long-handled brush and went to work.

Daryl went on, as usual, with her pep talk, telling the audience members they were the liveliest and most cooperative people she had ever worked with. She glanced back toward the stage, saw that the makeup artist had finished with Susannah, then she turned to the audience again.

"And so we begin," Daryl said. "Newt isn't here, but let's make him proud." For a moment, dead silence filled the room. Then the crew cheered and applauded, the audience joined in, and Daryl beamed. It seemed apparent to Kate that the cheers going up from the crew were not about making Newt proud. She was almost certain they were because he wasn't there to direct the segment.

But why was he was gone? Producer-directors just didn't do a "no-show," did they? Something didn't add up.

And what about the threats she'd heard against him? She considered each one. Then she considered the caked mud on the Miata tires.

Daryl called out, "Quiet on the set!"

Kate sat back and tried to relax, focusing her attention on Susannah's performance. Her friend bantered with the audience even as she showed them how to make her no-fail chocolate soufflé. She literally had them eating out of the palm of her hand.

Despite her jokes and hearty showmanship, Kate could tell Susannah worried about something. It was obvious by the way she glanced at the door leading to the foyer, the worried scrutiny she gave her spices as she measured each, even the sniff she gave the eggs as she cracked them.

Maybe no one else noticed. But Kate did.

As the taping continued, Kate better understood Susannah's nervousness. Someone forgot to turn on the oven. A key saucepan was missing. The electric mixer was stuck on its highest speed. Yet Kate had watched the preshow preparations with unblinking concentration. She hadn't noticed anything—or anyone—unusual.

Susannah handled each little glitch with humor and grace, and the audience loved her for it.

Then, almost as if on cue, Kisses started to snore. What

began as soft Chihuahua-size sleepy sighs rumbled into louder and louder full-blown, people-size snores.

From the stage, Susannah pointedly looked toward Kate with a quizzical frown.

Daryl put her hands on her hips and yelled, "Cut!" Then shielding her eyes from the bright stage lights, she turned to search the audience for the culprit.

Kate made a snap decision. "Let me have him," she whispered to Renee. "He needs some fresh air." And so did she.

When Kate gathered the little dog into her arms, he woke with a loud snort, then looked startled at his own noise. The audience laughed. Even Daryl chuckled.

"Well, now," Susannah said from where she was still standing at the kitchen-set counter. "I never thought I'd be upstaged by a dog. A sleeping dog at that."

As the audience laughed with Susannah, Kate led the Chihuahua from the studio by his jeweled leash.

She walked him around the parking lot for a few minutes, then caught herself meandering toward Susannah's Miata. Kisses fixed his gaze on the rear tire, but Kate nudged him toward a clump of autumn-brown grass.

While he sniffed his way through the grass, Kate stooped to have another look at the mud. The mud made of red clay.

Suddenly, it came to her where she'd seen it before.

"Come on, little fella," she said to Kisses. "We're going for a drive."

KATE SPED OUT of town, Kisses standing on her lap, ears perked, looking through the driver's side window. She had turned on Smith Street, knowing the red mud came from a

certain part of Copper Mill Creek where the creek mean-
dered west, creating short, rocky falls and lengthy pools.

Joe Tucker's house was in that same direction, five miles
out, but the place she had in mind was about a mile short of
Joe's place.

It took her only a few minutes to reach the turn off—a
dirt road that led to the creek. She and Paul had picnicked
there once after Joe pointed it out to them. She remembered
it as peaceful, the air filled with birdsong and bubbling brook
sounds.

She rounded a corner, now in full view of the place she
remembered.

There, just beyond a clump of willows and autumn-bare
trees, was the Hummer.

Kate's eyes filled. She didn't realize until now how much
she had hoped she was wrong.

This was the only place she knew of in Copper Mill
where the Miata could have picked up such substantial
amounts of this mud.

Susannah had been here.

Chapter Eight

At 4:13 AM, Kate's eyes flew open. Her sleep had been restless at best, and since midnight, she had spent more time tossing and turning than sleeping. After she found the Hummer, she'd called 911 immediately. As difficult as it was to stay away from the vehicle, she wasn't ready to intrude on what might be the scene of a crime.

Now she wondered if she should have taken the risk and checked out the Hummer. She knew the sheriff had launched an investigation after she called, but what if he—or his deputies—missed something important? With so much at stake, she should at least have taken a peek through the windows.

After Sheriff Roberts had called for the investigation, the hills and valleys around Copper Mill Creek had been combed by his staff, by volunteer search-and-rescue members from neighboring towns, by concerned citizens who just wanted to help, and by a few of the less disgruntled Taste crew members.

It was one of the biggest events to hit Copper Mill in years, and Kate suspected many of the searchers were looking for him not out of love but because they hoped for a bit of media attention. That assumed, of course, that the media got wind of the news—and Kate was certain they would.

But that wasn't what had kept her awake most of the night. She'd been thinking about Newt Keller himself. No matter how abominable the man had been to others, he didn't deserve whatever foul play that had apparently befallen him.

Kate swung her legs out of bed, grabbed her robe, and padded into the kitchen to make a cup of chamomile tea. She usually made coffee as soon as she got up, but caffeine was the last thing she needed when her brain was buzzing already. While she waited for the teakettle to heat, she leaned against the counter, arms folded.

She tried not to think about the three people she'd heard make threats against Keller, but she couldn't push them from her mind any longer. Birdie. Armand. And the one person she still couldn't bear to consider: Susannah . . . The teakettle rattled to a simmering boil, and Kate lifted it from the burner before its shrill whistle woke Paul. After pouring herself a steaming mug of tea, she carried it into the living room, flipped on the switch to the fireplace, and settled into her rocking chair with a sigh.

She bowed her head, praying for peace to flood her soul. How she needed it this morning! A verse from the Psalms came to her, and she whispered it as a prayer. "Let your unfailing love comfort me, just as you promised me . . ."

As was her custom every morning she prayed for Paul and his ministry, the Faith Briar parishioners, their children, and friends . . . and especially for Susannah. "Let your unfailing love comfort *her* this day, Lord," she whispered.

As she finished praying, her thoughts returned to her

friend. How well did she really know Susannah? Was she capable of carrying out her thinly veiled threats against Newt? What about the clumps of mud on her tires?

Kate rocked gently and sipped her tea, sick at heart that she even had to consider her friend's possible role in this dreadful twist of events. Sick at heart that she had to get to the truth about her prime suspect.

IT WAS WELL BEFORE DAWN when Kate turned the Honda into the hotel parking lot. A damp mist had settled close to the ground, and she pressed her lips together nervously, trying not to think about the ghost said to haunt the place. She'd left Paul a note, letting him know she had some investigating to do before breakfast. She flicked off the headlights and rolled silently to a halt beside Susannah's Miata. She needed a sample to compare to the mud at the creek where she found the Hummer.

After a quick glance around to make sure she was alone, Kate crept to the sports car to get a better look at the mud in the wheel wells.

As she knelt down beside the rear tire on the driver's side, she pulled a putty knife, a penlight, and a Ziploc baggie out of her jacket pocket. Then, holding the penlight in her mouth, she aimed the beam at the tire to retrieve the sample she was after.

Even in the dark of predawn, she could see that something was different.

Frowning, she directed the penlight beam along the wheel well. There was no mud on the car. Not even a speck!

Kate rocked back on her heels and aimed the beam at the front tire on the driver's side.

Clean. Shiny. Newly washed.

With a sigh, she stood and brushed off her hands. Why would Susannah go to the trouble to wash her car? Copper Mill didn't have a car wash, which meant she had to have hosed the car off herself, or hired someone to do it.

Still puzzling over what it could mean, she started to turn to head back to her car.

A hand touched her shoulder.

Her hair stood on end. She whirled around, heart thudding. Images of ghosts and flickering lights turned her knees to jelly in the split second before she completed the turn.

"Renee!" she breathed, relieved and irritated at the same time. "What are you doing here?"

Renee Lambert, dressed in black and wearing a photographer's vest with pockets for every possible sleuthing tool, held her finger to her lips. She wore a miner's headlamp, though, thankfully, it wasn't turned on.

"Shh," she mouthed. "We can't let anyone know we're here."

"My thoughts exactly," Kate whispered. "But you didn't answer my question. Why—"

Renee pointed to the path leading from the hotel to the creek. "I've been patrolling the area ever since we saw those spooky lights."

"You haven't been here all night, have you?"

"No, I stopped by at midnight to patrol the area, then I came back just before you arrived. You scared me to death with your little flashlight. I thought the ghost had returned."

"I didn't see your car."

She harrumphed. "You think I would leave it in plain view?" She tilted her head toward the *Grits 101* coach. "It's over there, behind the star coach."

"You haven't seen any more lights?"

Renee's shoulders slumped. "No."

Kate knew that Renee loved slipping around, spying on unsuspecting suspects. *Law and Order* was one of her favorite TV programs. Kate wouldn't have been surprised if Renee knew more police lingo and procedures than Sheriff Roberts did.

"What would you have done if you'd seen something?" Kate asked gently. Renee might be brusque and aggressive, but Kate worried about her. Renee considered herself no older than thirty-nine, but in reality, she was in her early seventies. She never complained, but Kate knew from the way she sometimes winced that the aches and pains of aging had begun to set in.

Renee sniffed. "I'd have gone to investigate, of course."

"Are you coming back for the taping this morning?"

"Wouldn't miss it. I want to see who looks the most guilt—" Her breath caught midword, and she whirled at the same instant the hair on the back of Kate's neck stood on end.

An unearthly sound carried toward them from the creek path. It was the same sound Kate had heard a few nights earlier: the light padding of footsteps.

But no one was on the path.

"Ghosts supposedly don't walk; they float," Kate whispered, then she realized how ridiculous that sounded and added, "If we believed in ghosts, that is."

A chilly wind whistled through the trees as the two women crept toward the creek. Kate shivered, wishing the fog would lift. The path leading away from the hotel was an eerie place to be in the pale light of dawn, especially when she could see only dark shadows of barren trees on either side. She pushed thoughts of what might be lurking behind them from her mind.

She took a few more steps, then stopped and blinked in surprise. She heard Renee halt a few steps behind her.

Just beyond a stand of trees a barely visible light pierced the dense fog.

It seemed more like a flickering glow than a flashlight.

Candlelight. Diffused because of the fog, but candlelight, just like the ghostly night the folks from Taste Network arrived.

"Do you see that?" she whispered to Renee. "It looks like someone is carrying a candle."

"Or some*thing*..." Renee whispered back. Her voice trembled.

Kate frowned and told herself for the hundredth time that she didn't believe in ghosts. "Okay," she said out loud, "I'm going to get to the bottom of this." She clicked on her penlight, broke into a trot, and headed down the path.

Behind her, Renee's footsteps sounded reluctantly slow at first, then sped to a scuttle.

"Hey, wait up," she puffed.

Kate rounded a corner. The fog was now thinning into eerie fingers that laced around the barren tree trunks. Kate could see the path several feet ahead and, beside it, the rushing creek... but nothing more.

No ghostly being. No being of *any* kind, human or otherwise.

With a sigh, she halted.

Renee caught up with her, still huffing and puffing.

"Whew," she breathed. "You really can move when you're motivated."

"A lot of good it did," Kate said, rubbing her arthritic knee while she scanned the brush around them. Then she frowned and peered into the mist. Ahead, by the creek, lay something that hadn't been there the first night she was led on the same wild-goose chase.

She squinted at the curious object and then headed toward it. Renee followed close behind.

"I think it's a boat," Kate said when they were closer. "A rowboat."

"Upside down," Renee said, stating the obvious. "*Hunh.*"

Kate trotted to the side of the boat, which was resting on the bank. It was light enough now to see the skid marks where someone must have dragged it from the water.

Kate walked around it, looking for footprints in the damp soil. At first it appeared there were none. Then to one side, an indentation caught her attention. She stooped to have a better look. It was a print, but it had been left by someone wearing slippers, ballet slippers with their distinct gathered-leather soles. Her daughters had worn them when they took ballet lessons years before. She knew them well.

She brushed off her hands and stood, studying the area around the rowboat.

The only other clue that someone had been there recently was a candle, partially spent, lying near the ballerina prints. It might have been there a while, or perhaps . . .

Kate stared at the candle for a moment, then stooped to pick it up. She pinched the wick between her thumb and forefinger and looked up at Renee.

"The wick is still warm."

Renee's eyes widened. She looked frantically around, then whispered, "The ghost is still here."

Chapter Nine

A few minutes before nine that same morning, Kate returned to the hotel. This time the parking lot was alive with media activity. News vans from network TV affiliates out of Chattanooga and Nashville were parked in front of the hotel. Satellite dishes had sprung up like mushrooms atop the vans, and reporters were milling about the front of the hotel.

Before Kate reached the hotel entrance, two reporters asked for her comments on Newt Keller's disappearance.

She declined.

As she entered the foyer, she spotted a distraught-looking Sybil standing by the reception desk and went over to her.

The hotel manager shuddered. "I thought the ghost stories were bad enough. Now this." She shook her head slowly. "I don't know if we'll ever recover."

"It'll blow over," Kate said, trying to encourage her. "These things always do."

"If Keller is found alive and well," Sybil muttered.

"From what I understand, the authorities don't think it's anything more than an abduction."

A reporter holding a wireless microphone trotted toward them, a cameraman on her heels. Before Sybil could get away, the mike was thrust toward her, and with camera rolling, the pretty young reporter chirped, "Someone from your reservations staff told us that Newt Keller was staying in room 213, which is the same site as a 1929 murder. In light of the news that the Hamilton Springs is haunted, wasn't it risky to assign him—or anyone—to that room? And now he's disappeared, and rumor has it that blood was found in his SUV. That's quite a coincidence, don't you think? Any comment?"

Sybil took a deep breath. "No comment."

Kate blinked, trying to take everything in. Why hadn't Sybil told her that Newt Keller was booked in room 213, especially since Kate had mentioned that the master key wouldn't open the door? Not to mention that supposedly, no one else was even staying in that wing?

The reporter thrust the mike closer to Sybil. "Surely you have something to say about this . . ."

Sensing Sybil's extreme discomfort, Kate stepped forward to let her off the hook. "Until the authorities have conducted their investigation, it isn't appropriate for anyone but the police to comment. Out of respect for that process—"

She was interrupted by a commotion across the foyer. Before she could finish her statement, the perky reporter and her cameraman scampered toward a swarm of other reporters and camerapeople. Standing on a makeshift dais were two of the three stars of Taste Network—Nicolette Pascal and Birdie Birge. Daryl Gallagher stood between them.

All three looked and sounded appropriately somber, though Kate suspected if she stepped closer, she might detect a glad-to-be-in-the-limelight glint in their eyes. In front of them stood a mix of media and studio audience members, who were waiting for the taping to begin.

Copper Mill residents were scattered around the foyer. Renee and Caroline were seated on a sofa near the fireplace, and LuAnne and Millie were standing with Joe Tucker near the entrance to the kitchen set. LuAnne had arranged for another waitress to cover her shift at the diner, and Millie said she could stay only a half day because she had some filing to do at the church. Eli, Willy, and Sam couldn't make it because of work. Livvy had called Kate earlier saying she needed to finalize details about the Joel St. Nicklaus book signing and would join Kate later.

All around her, Kate could hear snatches of conversation, and the word that cropped up the most was *abduction*. She shivered. Surely such a thing hadn't happened to Newt. He might be abrasive but why would someone want to hurt him? What would be the gain?

Her gaze traveled to Susannah, who stood off to one side, away from the crowd. Though she was dressed in her chef's uniform, she looked anything but ready for the morning's taping. Her hair was disheveled, her face lined with worry, her shoulders slumped as if they carried the weight of the universe.

Kate's heart went out to her. She put aside all thoughts that Susannah might be involved in Newt Keller's disappearance and headed toward her. Reporters were firing questions at the three women on the dais, who were obviously pros at handling such things. They were poised, engaging, and appropriately grave. Their body language said they had long been waiting for this moment in the media spotlight.

As soon as Kate reached Susannah, she wrapped an arm around her shoulders. "You look like you could use a friend."

Susannah nodded, her eyes filling.

Just then, Sheriff Alan Roberts swept through the door, glowering when he spotted the swarm of reporters. Deputy Skip Spencer followed on his heels.

The crowd parted like the Red Sea as Sheriff Roberts and Skip strode toward the dais.

The sheriff looked out at the crowd. His tone was no-nonsense when he spoke. "The Q and A is over for now, folks. A briefing will be scheduled for later in the day to apprise you of any developments. In the meantime, I'd appreciate some breathing room to interview the network cast and crew." A couple of news reporters tried to shoot off a few more questions, but Skip herded them through the exit and into the parking lot.

Kate smiled. It wasn't often that Skip could carry out a command and not bungle it in the sheriff's presence.

"As you know," Sheriff Roberts was saying to those who remained, "Newt Keller was last seen at the Country Diner on Wednesday, having lunch alone. His vehicle was found yesterday morning about four miles from town, abandoned. Blood was discovered on the upholstery, which leads us to believe that foul play may be involved. Because of the circumstances, I need to speak with everyone Newt Keller was in contact with since his arrival Tuesday evening."

He paused, frowning. "It's been reported that several threats were made against Mr. Keller before he disappeared. I'm speaking to the cast and crew of the network here, but if anyone else has anything to say, you need to tell us now. As my deputy and I conduct the interviews, I encourage you to be forthcoming. Names have been turned in to our office, but it will go easier for you if you tell us what you know. If you don't tell us here, maybe a trip to the Sheriff's Office will help jog your memory."

After a few more instructions about how the interviews would be conducted, Sheriff Roberts stepped down from the dais and headed toward two long tables that had been set up in the foyer. He took a seat at the nearest table, and Skip took a seat at the other. Kate hesitated, agonizing as she thought through her options. Should she tell the sheriff about the mud on Susannah's Miata? She blinked back the threat of tears. She couldn't turn her friend in without further investigation.

Susannah squeezed Kate's hand. "I'm glad you're here," she said. "I couldn't get through all this without you."

Kate let out a pent-up sigh. She could always call the sheriff later. For now, her friend needed her support.

Susannah squeezed Kate's hand again, then walked toward the sheriff. Kate watched as Susannah spoke with him. She kept her demeanor lighthearted, almost as if she were bantering with an audience member. The sheriff looked anything but lighthearted. As the conversation proceeded, his scowl deepened. And as he took notes, his tight-lipped expression made Kate's heart skip a beat.

Susannah's expression changed too. By the time the interview was over, she looked pale and drawn.

KATE SPENT THE REST of the morning at the library, doing research on the Hamilton Springs Hotel. Near the end of her two hours online, Kate glanced up and spotted Livvy coming her way. Kate smiled as her friend sat down in the swivel chair next to her.

"How about lunch?" Livvy offered.

"I'd love it. Diner?"

Livvy nodded. "I've got a hankering for a bowl of chicken-and-dumpling soup. It's that kind of day." She glanced at the computer screen. "Did you find anything?"

Kate sat back. "I had no idea there was any truth to all this ghost business."

Livvy raised an eyebrow and laughed. "You mean that the ghost is real after all?"

Kate chuckled with her. "Not quite. I meant there's a historical basis for the ghost stories. This morning, a reporter asked Sybil if she had purposely put Newt Keller in room 213, the same room where someone was killed in 1929."

"And . . . ?"

"A person did die in that room. Strangely, Joel St. Nicklaus didn't include that little tidbit in his book, the room number I mean. He also took a bit of literary license when he said that someone was killed in that wing of the hotel, implying it was murder. In the information I've found, it wasn't murder at all."

"I'm not surprised," Livvy said. "But at least he's up front about it. I've seen him interviewed. He admits that he fictionalized most of the original stories to make them more interesting." Livvy shook her head. "What some authors will do to sell books . . ."

Kate chuckled. "The problem with fictionalized nonfiction is that you've got to sleuth your way through the material to figure out what's true and what's not."

Livvy grinned. "If anybody can do that, it's you. I would think you've gone through *Famous Haunts* with a fine-tooth comb."

"It's more like sifting flour—sifting out the untruths and innuendos until you can see the facts," Kate said with a sigh. "What I can figure so far to be true is that Precious McFie was jilted just days before her wedding. She came from Nashville high society, a debutante, and her wedding was to be the event of the year. When her fiancé ran off with another woman, Precious was scandalized. There wasn't even enough time for her parents to notify guests that the wedding was canceled. She came here from Nashville and booked room 213 at the hotel. Of course, it was called the Copper Creek Hotel back then.

"Later, it was reported that she walked up and down the path by the creek from midnight to dawn for several nights, in her wedding gown. Winter had arrived in full force that year, and the air turned bitter cold, with sleet and hail and terrible winds. She caught pneumonia and died in her room a few days later. A doctor was called, but it was too late."

The two women stood. Kate gathered her pen and notebook and dropped them into her handbag. As they walked down the stairs to the first floor, Kate continued. "A big deal was made over the fact that she died in room 213 on November thirteenth. Legend has it that every year around that time, a ghost dressed as a bride haunts the room where she died, the second-floor wing where we've seen the flickering lights, the parking lot, and the path along the creek."

They reached the exit door downstairs, and Livvy pushed it open.

"There's something unsettling about the hotel assigning Newt Keller that same room," Kate said as she stepped outside.

"Could it have been just a coincidence, or an oversight?" Livvy fell in beside Kate as they crossed Main Street on foot, heading toward the diner.

"That wing isn't usually available for guests. Maybe for overflow, if need be. But from what I gather, no one goes up there except the housekeepers. It doesn't make sense that a guest would be assigned to that room. I don't think it's an accident."

They reached the diner and were seated. Because LuAnne had taken the week off for the Taste tapings, her stand-in took their orders. With her fair skin and multitude of freckles, she looked all of sixteen, but she was friendly and efficient. They ordered two bowls of soup and a basket of cornbread.

"How are the plans for the book signing coming along?"

Livvy sighed. "Not well. During the last planning meeting, the Caspers lined up in front of the library, trying to keep the Ghostbusters from picketing."

"Who in the world are the Ghostbusters?"

Livvy gave her a wan smile. "Caspers believe in ghosts and, for some reason, want everyone else to believe too. The Ghostbusters are convinced that ghosts do not exist, and both sides have picked this up as some sort of cause."

Kate slumped back in the booth. "What will this do to your signing? Do you think people will stay away?"

"I hope not. I got an e-mail from Joel St. Nicklaus this morning. He's bringing a professional storyteller with him. Someone with Southern roots who can tell a famous ghost story with theatrical flair."

"And the Ghostbusters are trying to get you to cancel, I suppose."

Livvy nodded. "You've got it." She leaned forward. "Kate, what do you think I should do? I already said yes to Joel St. Nicklaus. It's a rare occasion when a professional story-teller comes to Copper Mill, and I'm excited about it. But if the Caspers and Ghostbusters picket the event . . ." She shrugged. "It'll become a circus. Laughable. I can't have that."

"We need to figure out a way to stop them," Kate said, frowning in thought.

Livvy shrugged. "That's the problem. I don't know what any of us can do to stop it."

"What about getting both sides together—?"

Before Kate could answer, the waitress brought two steaming bowls of soup and a basket of cornbread, then asked if there would be anything else. After they said no, the young woman hesitated as if uncertain of something. Then she said, "What you were talking about just now . . ."

Livvy and Kate looked up, spoons poised above their bowls.

"Well, my grandma's a Casper."

"Oh?" said Livvy.

The two women put down their spoons.

"She swears a ghost lives in her house and roams around

at night while she and Grandpa are sleeping. Grandpa says it's utter foolishness, but Grandma insists her ghost is real. She says Sophronia is a friendly ghost who wouldn't hurt a flea. Just roams around, room to room, floorboards creaking. Sometimes Sophronia rearranges furniture or puts dishes in different cupboards during the night. That's the only thing Grandma doesn't like about her ghost."

"How does she know the ghost's name is Sophronia?" Kate asked.

"That was the name of Grandma's granny, who was born in that same house. Died there too. Grandma says the ghost never told her its name, but she says she feels the kinship in her bones."

"And your grandpa is a Ghostbuster?" Livvy asked, then lifted her spoon to her mouth.

The young woman nodded. "He says Grandma sleepwalks —gets out of her wheelchair by herself and everything. He swears she does all those things herself, and just doesn't remember."

"Has he stayed up to watch so he knows for sure?" Kate stirred her soup to cool it, then slid her spoon into its fragrant depths.

The young waitress laughed and tucked her pencil over one ear. "The one night Grandpa tried to stay awake, nothing happened. He fell asleep in his recliner just before dawn. When he woke up a couple hours later, he was covered by an old quilt that Grandma had on display in the parlor with her Granny's treadle sewing machine. Grandma was still asleep upstairs in their bedroom and swore she hadn't been up during the night."

Someone called for a coffee refill, and the girl hollered she'd be right there.

"What about you?" Kate asked. "Do you believe in ghosts?"

The waitress looked down at her nametag and patted it gently. "Have to. I'm named after my great-great grandma Sophronia." She looked up and grinned. "But I go by Sophie." Then she winked. "Sometimes I do a little ghosting myself when I sleep over at my grandparents' place."

She started to head across the room for the coffeepot, then she paused and looked back. "Grandma and I will be at the library when that author comes to town."

"How about your grandfather?" Livvy asked, looking worried.

"Yep, he'll be there too. But as a protestor."

"With a sign?" Kate asked.

"Of course. All their signs have little ghosts with red circles around 'em. You've seen those before, right?"

Kate and Livvy nodded.

"And that's not all. Some of the Caspers plan to come in costume, hoping it will give their cause some publicity."

"You're kidding!" Livvy gaped, and Kate knew what was going through her mind. The event was turning into a big top right before her eyes.

"But Grandma said they're going to update the look a bit. Instead of white sheets, she and her Casper friends are planning to wear patterns—stripes, plaids, and florals."

As Sophie headed for the coffeepot, Kate and Livvy looked at each other. "I know this is serious, and you're very concerned, Livvy, but"—the corner of her mouth twitched— "if they actually do this . . ."

"I can picture it now," Livvy said, biting her lips to keep from laughing. Then a giggle erupted, followed by another. They looked at each other again and cracked up.

After a moment of nearly breathless laughter, Livvy's expression softened. "We can't let this happen, Kate. But for the life of me, I can't figure out how to stop it."

Kate reached for Livvy's hand. "Seriously, Livvy. We'll think of something. The floral sheets might strike us as funny, but the repercussions for the library—and for you—aren't. We'll find a way to stop it."

"I know we will," Livvy said, and dipped her spoon into her soup. But her expression didn't match her words.

The women had just finished their meal when Kate's cell phone buzzed.

She checked the caller ID before lifting the phone to her ear. Susannah Applebaum.

"Hi, Suse—" she began, but Susannah cut her off.

"Kate," her friend whispered. Her voice trembled as if she'd been crying. "I'm in trouble. I need your help."

Chapter Ten

Saturday morning, Kate rose early and headed into the living room for her devotions. Her heart was heavy as she thought about Susannah. Today of all days, she needed more bolstering than a strong cup of early morning coffee could provide.

She opened her Bible to Psalm 37 and read through the entire chapter, then she returned to the verses that seemed to speak to her heart: *Trust in the Lord and do good ... delight yourself in the Lord and he shall give you the desires of your heart ... commit your way to the Lord ... Rest in the Lord and wait patiently for him ... do not fret ...*

Her eyes opened wide as she focused on the words *trust, delight, commit, rest ...* and especially, *do not fret.*

She smiled, realizing that these verses were sent straight from God's heart to hers for this day. If ever she needed to trust God in the circumstances around her, it was now.

She wasn't very good at waiting patiently, and she was terrible at trying not to fret. But the one thing she could do, perhaps above all the others on the list, was to delight in him, no matter the seriousness of the circumstances around her, no matter her concerns about Susannah, Livvy and the library, or about the mystery she was trying to solve.

After spending time in prayer, she stood to go into the
kitchen to put on the coffee. A gentle peace settled into her
soul, and she leaned against the counter and whispered,
"Thank you."

Because Paul was still asleep, Kate decided to try out
Susannah's recipe for brownies—and to think over the
new wrinkle in the mystery surrounding Newt Keller's
disappearance.

She pulled out the ingredients: four squares of unsweet-
ened chocolate, unsalted butter, eggs, sugar, flour, and cream
cheese.

As the chocolate squares and butter melted on the stove,
she pondered Susannah's dilemma. Kate had immediately
invited her over when she called the day before, even letting
her know she was welcome to stay with them until all the
trouble blew over.

But Susannah didn't want to appear afraid, so she opted
to stay at the hotel. But she did join Kate and Paul for dinner
and seemed heartened by Paul's prayer for her during grace,
as well as their conversation later over coffee and cookies at
the table.

Kate hadn't been surprised to hear that Sheriff Roberts was
considering her a prime suspect and had ordered her not to
leave town. Kate hadn't been the only one to hear the threats,
and there was a possibility others had noticed the mud on her
tires.

But Susannah was devastated. "I would never hurt
Newt," she said. "I couldn't—not him or anyone else. But I
know the circumstantial evidence against me—my threats,
the fact that I disappeared the same afternoon he did . . ." She

shook her head. "I can't help feeling someone is behind this, that it's a set up."

"Where did you go that afternoon?" Kate asked.

"On a drive. I was so upset; I admit it. Newt can really get under my skin. And he embarrassed me that day—in front of the studio audience, in front of the crew. I was ready to just walk off the set, cancel the show, get out of my contract, the works."

Susannah took a bite of her cookie, chewing thoughtfully. "Hmm, these are wonderful, Kate." She reached for another.

"Did the sheriff mention other suspects?" Kate asked. "I heard other threats, surely those people came forward."

Susannah nodded. "He did say that I wasn't the only one overheard making threats."

"Anyone who works with Newt will tell you that it's an understatement to say he's not well liked," Susannah said. "Anyone could have been involved in his disappearance. But I'm the only person who disappeared at precisely the same time he did."

Kate had to ask. "Why did you wash off the mud?"

Susannah gave her a sharp look. "You noticed?" Then she laughed lightly. "You've always been one for details."

But she didn't answer Kate's question.

She helped with dishes, thanked them for dinner, and zoomed off in her silver Miata, leaving Kate and Paul standing on the porch, arm in arm, with more questions than they'd had before she arrived.

Kate turned her attention back to the brownies as she continued musing about the events of the past few days. The chocolate and butter had melted, so she stirred in the dry ingredients.

Something had been bothering her since she heard about the producer's disappearance. But she'd been so caught up in her friend's complicity that she hadn't dwelt much on the major piece of evidence pointing to foul play: the blood on the SUV's upholstery.

And the rumors about Newt being abducted? Why was everyone going in that direction? She stopped stirring, spoon hovering, and thought about it for a minute.

If it had been an abduction, there had to be a reason for it. What would someone possibly want in exchange for Newt Keller? Might a rival network want him out of the picture temporarily? Or maybe a disgruntled business partner?

A new thought flitted around the edges of her brain. What if one or more of the Taste Network employees just wanted to enjoy a week without Newt? Maybe they were in cahoots, and it wasn't foul play at all. But kidnapping was still a crime, punishable by years in prison.

Her thoughts turned to Susannah and all she stood to lose if she was involved in such a crime. Kate gave the chocolate mixture another stir as she thought about the Hummer and the reddish mud around the wheels of Susannah's Miata.

Was it possible the Hummer was still where she had found it? It was a crime scene, and only two days since the SUV had been found. Maybe she could get out to the site before the Hummer was towed away.

She quickly poured the brownie batter into a buttered pan, then swirled in the cream-cheese mixture. Baking could wait.

Paul shuffled around the corner in his slippers, tying his robe, just as Kate was heading out the door.

She gave him a quick good-morning kiss. "Do you think the Hummer might still be by the creek?"

He blinked in surprise. "You're heading out there right now?"

She smiled. "You know me and those ladybugs I get in my bonnet."

Paul laughed. "Ladybugs? I thought they were bees."

"Mine are a gentler, quieter version. More like ladybugs."

He was still grinning when he said, "I'm not sure the Hummer will be there. It may have been towed to an impound garage in Pine Ridge by now. Probably depends on if the crime people are finished with their investigation. You could call the sheriff to find out."

"I'll take a chance," she said. "I've got something I need to check out—something that may have been overlooked."

"Those crime scene folks are very thorough..." Then he laughed. "I should know better by now. You have a knack for finding things everyone else misses. Just be careful, Katie."

"Aren't I always?"

Paul sighed. "Not as careful as I'd like."

Kate waved good-bye to Paul as she backed out of the driveway. When she reached the intersection at Smoky Mountain Road and Mountain Laurel, she took a right. Then she took another right onto Smith Street and headed northeast. She turned again when she spotted the dirt road that led to the creek.

The weather that morning was bright and sunny, not at all like the November weather that had taken Precious McFie's life.

Off in the distance, Kate spotted a yellow glint in the morning sun. The Hummer! She pressed on the accelerator.

She passed a stand of willows, and there before her sat the Hummer. Right next to it was a sheriff's department black-and-white SUV. Not too far away, a lawn chair had been placed in the shade of a willow tree. A thermos of coffee sat beside it.

But there was no sign of the sheriff or his deputy. Only a long strand of police tape strung from a couple of trees in front of the Hummer.

Kate fished around in her pocket for a pair of pop-up disposable gloves she'd brought along. She normally used them for chopping things like onions and garlic, but they were perfect for crime-scene sleuthing. She pulled on the gloves, then headed over to the Hummer.

She opened the door on the driver's side and, squinting, looked for the dried blood.

The upholstery was a buttery-hued leather, and as she bent closer, the bloodstains she'd heard about were easily visible. It appeared that when the blood was fresh, it had dripped down from about the level of Newt Keller's neck and along the back of the seat. Another smear shot off to the left as if the body had been pulled out of the vehicle.

She made a mental note to ask if a DNA test had shown any results. Blood type would be good to know too, especially if Keller's type was rare.

Kate next went around to the passenger side and opened the door. She opened the glove box and peered inside, but the gaping space was empty. So was the center console. She reached under the seat and fished around but came up empty there as well.

She carefully examined the rear seating area, the carpeted floor, the headliner. Nothing unusual.

She backed out of the rear of the vehicle, stepped back, and reached for the door. Just before she pressed it closed, something caught her eye. Leaning across the passenger seat, she peered into the CD player. Usually, the protective flap was down, fitting snugly in place when the player wasn't in use. But the flap was propped open. With something small lodged inside the slit. Maybe a pen or pencil . . .

She frowned and leaned close enough to reach the player with her right hand. She placed her gloved index finger on one side of the object and her middle finger on the other.

The object didn't budge. She rocked it gently back and forth, then tried to pull again. It seemed frozen in place.

She pulled back her hand and stared at the end of the object, the only visible part. She narrowed her eyes. The object seemed familiar, but she couldn't figure out where she'd seen something like that before.

"Hey, what's going on here?" The gruff voice behind her made her start, then bump her head in her hurry to extricate herself from the Hummer.

"Oh, it's you, Missus Hanlon," Skip Spencer said. "But what are you doing here? This is a crime scene, and nobody's supposed to get near this vehicle. I'm afraid I must ask you to back away from the door."

"I just wanted to have a look for myself. And I think I've found something." She started for the Hummer again.

"Please, ma'am. You'll contaminate the crime scene."

"Don't you want to see what I found?"

"The investigators have been over the vehicle with a fine-tooth comb. I'm sure they found everything they needed." He looked at his watch. "The tow truck will be here in another few minutes to take the vehicle to the impound garage, so I'll have to ask you to keep your distance, Missus Hanlon."

Kate sighed. "It's there," she said, pointing to the CD player. "Can you see how it's propped open? This may be something important. If you won't let me investigate, you should at least take a look."

Skip sauntered over to the SUV and leaned across the passenger's seat. "Oh yeah, I do see something."

The clock was ticking, and Kate wasn't about to let the Hummer get away before she was finished. "I've got gloves on. Let me pull it out."

Skip hesitated, obviously weighing law-enforcement procedure against Kate's knack for finding new evidence, something he'd seen firsthand.

"Well, as long as you keep your gloves on, I guess it'll be all right. Sheriff Roberts assigned me the job of keeping watch over the evidence to make sure no one tampers with it, and I intend to carry out my duties to the best of my ability."

Kate was only half listening as she tried to free the object in the player. Then she blinked as the realization hit. Of course she knew what it was. She also knew that if she turned it flatside down, it would easily slide out of the CD player.

It did.

She gingerly held it up for Skip to see.

"A pocketknife," he said in awe. "How'd you know it was in there?"

Kate didn't answer. She was too busy examining the Swiss Army Knife. It was just like Paul's, one of the smallest designs made. One of the least obtrusive for a man to carry in his pocket.

Kate carefully held it up to the sunlight.

"Do you think that's the weapon the perpetrators used?" Skip asked.

"I don't know, but there's dried blood on the blade."

Chapter Eleven

K ate called Susannah as soon as she arrived home. "Did Newt Keller ever use a pocketknife when you were around him?"

"Oh yes. He carries it all the time. He's obsessive about his fingernails. Always trimming and filing. The knife he carries has tiny scissors, a file, and, of course, a couple of blades."

"Have you, by chance, ever seen him loan it to someone else?"

"He would never do that. He's also got this thing about germs. A bit over the top with that too. He even carries around his own tasting fork; he refuses to use a perfectly clean studio utensil." She hesitated. "Why do you ask?"

"Just an angle I'm working on."

They chatted for a few more minutes about the next taping, which was scheduled for Monday.

Just before they said their good-byes, Kate invited Susannah to come to church with her the following day.

Susannah seemed genuinely pleased and accepted the invitation.

Paul came in just as Kate hung up the phone.

"You're smiling ear to ear . . . You must be closer to connecting the dots."

She laughed. "Actually, I was smiling because Susannah's coming to Faith Briar tomorrow. She just accepted my invitation."

"That's great. Shall we have her over for lunch after?"

"Or maybe take her out?"

"There's always the Country Diner."

"I think she'd like that. She told me her favorite food is a good cheeseburger, with fries and all the fixin's. The diner has the best around."

SUSANNAH CAUSED QUITE A STIR the next morning when she zoomed into the church parking lot in her little Miata. Standing at the entrance, Kate waved, then headed over to greet her friend.

The previous afternoon, Kate had mentioned to Renee that Susannah would be attending Faith Briar. Renee had quickly gotten together an impromptu welcoming committee of a dozen or so parishioners, who were now standing at the front of the church, smiling at Kate and Susannah as they approached.

Renee stepped forward as if to formally welcome Susannah. Kisses trotted behind her on his jeweled leash, then sat down and stared up at Susannah. But Renee just stood there, her mouth moving, but no sound coming out.

For the first time since Kate had known Renee, the woman seemed at a loss for words. She was starstruck.

Susannah handled the situation with grace. She gathered

a startled Renee into a hug, then stood back and beamed at her. "I don't know if you realize how photogenic you are, but I've seen the tapes of my show, and you're beautiful."

Renee tilted her chin upward and patted her hair. "Well, yes. I've been told that before."

Susannah didn't miss a beat. She turned to the others who'd attended the tapings and said complimentary things to each.

"I wish all of you could attend every taping I do. It's too bad Atlanta is so far away. Wait till you see the real show. Y'all are simply great."

They made their way into the church, Kate feeling a bit like the Pied Piper. She escorted Susannah down to the front of the sanctuary, with the welcoming committee following and settling in around them as they sat down.

Susannah caught Kate's eye and grinned. It was obvious she loved the enthusiastic reception. It struck Kate then that God was using the welcoming committee to show Susannah how much she was loved and accepted—without judgment, without question. Their love was a reflection of his love; and that day, that morning, it was a gift from his heart to Susannah's. The funny thing was, they set out to greet her as fans and probably didn't know how God was using their admiration.

Kate sat back in awe as Sam played one of her favorite hymns, "His Eye Is on the Sparrow." God had used the ordinary folks at Faith Briar once again to touch someone's heart in an extraordinary way.

"Do you remember the words to this song?" she whispered to Susannah.

When Susannah turned, Kate saw tears in her eyes.

Susannah nodded. "I haven't thought of it in years. . . .

'Let not your heart be troubled, his tender word I hear, and resting on his goodness, I lose my doubts and fears...'"

Paul's sermon on taking courage in troubled times couldn't have been more perfectly suited for Susannah, yet Kate knew he'd been working on it long before he knew she would be attending.

"When you go through troubled times, consider that you are in training," Paul said toward the end of the sermon. "Stop for a moment and think about your challenges from a different perspective: consider dealing with adversity as strength training for your spirit, in much the same way lifting weights builds strong bones or jogging aerobically exercises the cardiovascular system.

"A long-distance runner pushes her body beyond what she thinks she can endure. Yet when she reaches her goal, her months or years of training make her trials worthwhile."

Then he stopped and looked out over the congregation. "Though it may be difficult in your present circumstances, rejoice and welcome the challenges ahead. Know that God is with you and will give you strength each step of the way."

As Paul read from Isaiah 43, Susannah pulled a small notebook and pen from her purse and jotted down the verses:

Do not be afraid, for I have ransomed you. I have called you by name; you are mine. When you go through deep waters and great trouble, I will be with you. When you go through rivers of difficulty, you will not drown! When you walk through the fire of oppression, you will not be burned up—the flames will not consume you.

After the service, Susannah gave Kate a hug. "This was the best gift you could have given me."

"HALF OF THE TASTE NETWORK IS HERE," Susannah said as they stepped out of the car in front of the diner. She cast a worried glance at the cars parked on both sides of the street.

Paul clicked the locks on the Honda and fell into step with the two women. But before reaching the door, Paul turned and asked, "Would you rather go someplace else? We can, you know."

Susannah hesitated, then smiled at them both. "I admit this is the first day I've left my room, but I decided this morning I'll have to face my colleagues sooner or later. It might as well be sooner. Besides, I'm not the only suspect. The sheriff wouldn't divulge any specifics, but I would bet there are other network people who are as nervous as I am about all this."

Back on the job for the coming week, LuAnne met them at the door, all smiles when she saw Susannah, then ushered them to a corner booth. Without asking, she poured three mugs of coffee, then slipped into the booth next to Kate.

"I want to tell you, honey," she said to Susannah, "*Sumptuous Chocolates* is the best thing on the tube. I wouldn't miss it for all the tea in Chi—" She laughed. "Make that all the cocoa beans in Brazil."

"Well, thank you," Susannah said. She took a sip of coffee, looked startled, and reached for the cream and sugar. The diner's coffee was sometimes a smidge too strong and bitter.

"We've got a lot of Tasties here today," LuAnne said, putting on her glasses and looking around the room. "Over there's that little French gal—what's her name?"

"Nicolette Pascal," Susannah filled in.

"Oh yes. I wouldn't tell her so, but of you three, I go for your show. I love that *Grits 101* gal—"

"Birdie Birge," Susannah filled in again.

"That's right, Birdie. Well, now, before I started watchin' her, I thought it was in the genes to fix 'em right. We Southern gals just instinctively know how to do it, know what I mean? I said to myself, 'Why should I listen to someone tell me what I already know how to do?'" She leaned across the table and lowered her voice. "Then mercy me, I found out that she does know a thing or two about grits. And you can tell her I said so."

Susannah smiled. "I think you should tell her yourself."

"But . . ." She paused dramatically. "There's somethin' I noticed recently about those two other chefs."

Kate exchanged glances with Paul, then held up a hand to stop the gossip LuAnne was about to spill. She was too late.

"They were talking about the tapings, their heads close together like it was some secret. Well, whenever anyone does that on my shift, it's my policy to step closer and hover with the coffeepot, if you know what I mean."

"I think we're all guilty of being one-note Johnnies," Susannah said. "When we're taping, that's the only thing on our minds. . . ."

LuAnne raised a brow. "They were talking about one chef stealing another chef's dessert recipes to use on her show."

Susannah looked startled and sat forward. "Did they mention names?"

"Yes, they did, honey—"

Before she could finish, the table of Taste crew members called to LuAnne to bring the coffeepot for a refill.

She waved a hand to the crew, then grinned at Susannah, Paul, and Kate. "First things first. Y'all want to order?"

After they ordered their cheeseburgers and fries, and

LuAnne had bustled off, Susannah told Paul how much she had enjoyed the church service, especially his sermon. But as they moved onto other subjects, she became more and more distracted, glancing toward the other chefs' table. Kate half expected Susannah to excuse herself and confront them, but it turned out she didn't need to.

When their cheeseburgers arrived and they had taken their first bites, Nicolette and Birdie stopped by their table on their way to the door.

After they exchanged pleasantries, Susannah got right to the point. "I understand you're worried about one of the Taste chefs stealing a dessert recipe." Smiling, she kept her tone pleasant. "I thought it might be appropriate to clear the air. Since there are only three of us, the obvious target of your suppositions is me."

Birdie held up her hands. "Hey, I didn't have anything to do with it. Remember I do grits, not chocolates. You two are the chocolate artisans par excellence."

"Darling, you are simply too sensitive." Nicolette stepped closer, speaking in her soft French accent, and fluttered her fingers. "I simply pointed out that the tiramisu you plan to make at tomorrow's taping is identical to mine."

"We've long been in competition with each other," Susannah said. "You've gone to a lot of trouble in the past to gain an advantage, and it's mostly been a friendly rivalry. But this . . . this accusation goes too far. I developed my recipe after weeks of experimentation. I've never seen your recipe or read it in a cookbook, on the Internet, or anywhere else. Besides, you do French fusion—chocolate isn't really your thing."

Nicolette leaned closer. "Cheri, you may think you've got a corner on the chocolate market, but you don't. Do you assume the French don't like chocolate? Or Southerners?" She laughed, a short, brittle sound.

Susannah didn't answer.

"Ooh la la," Nicolette said with another flutter of her fingers. "Who knows where we pick up our ideas? Sometimes I think it's in the air. Go ahead and use my recipe, darling. I certainly would never accuse you publicly of plagiarism."

"But in private?" Susannah's voice was almost a whisper. She had gone very pale.

"Of course, I meant that too," Nicolette said. "I'll never tell a soul. And now, darlings, I really must be on my way. I'll see you at the taping tomorrow." She blew them all a kiss, then turned to walk to the door with Birdie.

Nicolette's walk was as graceful as a ballerina's, and nearly every male in the diner watched her leave.

"I should have kept my mouth shut," Susannah said with a sigh. "But it didn't seem fair that I couldn't come to my own defense." She shrugged. "A lot of good it did. Nicolette still thinks I've nabbed one of her recipes."

Kate studied her friend for a moment, then said, "I read something on the Internet about the same accusations. . . ."

Susannah flushed and let her gaze drift away from Kate's. "I know there are rumors out there—completely unjustified, unfounded, but I don't know who started them or why."

"Hey, those people who love and follow your show will know the truth," Kate said. "Your passion for your recipes is evident, and that can only come from the heart, not from plagiarizing someone else's work. People know that."

Susannah smiled and shook her head slowly. "I don't know what tomorrow will bring, but you two sure made today a lot more bearable."

Paul's smile was filled with a gentle kindness, and he patted Susannah's hand. "We're here for you, Susannah. Anytime you need us, just call or stop by."

She nodded her thanks. "You two are the greatest." She smiled at Kate. "And you know that song . . . 'His Eye Is on the Sparrow'?"

Kate nodded.

"It's been playing over and over in my head since I heard it this morning. But I can't remember the last few lines."

Kate gave Susannah's hand a squeeze, then softly spoke the words. "'When song gives place to sighing, when hope within me dies, I draw closer to him, from care he sets me free . . .'"

"'His eye is on the sparrow, and I know he's watching me,'" Susannah finished. "If there's one thing I need to remember for the rest of my life—providing I can get through the next few days—it's that." She glanced down at her round frame and laughed. "Who would ever have thought I'd see myself as a sparrow?" When she looked up again, there were tears in her eyes. "But I do."

Chapter Twelve

Kate woke with a start. Something was troubling her, nagging at her as being important, but she didn't know what it was. A ghost of a dream still flickered behind her eyelids. But as she tried to recapture the nebulous images, the dream retreated into those foggy recesses of her brain where such things seem to reside.

She lifted the clock from her bedside table and squinted at its face: 5:15. Enough time for a quick snooze. Or she could spend the extra time in her favorite chair, praying and reading a passage of Scripture before Paul got up. She decided the latter would do her more good.

She grabbed her robe and slipped it on, then found her slippers. As she padded toward the kitchen to put on the coffee, her thoughts went immediately to Newt Keller's disappearance and everything related to it: the threats made against him, the Hummer and the bloodstains, the pocket-knife he never let anyone else use.

If he hadn't let anyone borrow it, could it have been taken forcibly from him and used as a weapon to get him to cooperate with his abductor? If that was the case, his abductor would have to be strong enough to overpower him ... or maybe there was more than one abductor involved in the crime. Kate didn't think a lone female could pull it off.

She was missing something, something big. She had her theories, but that's all they were, theories as nebulous as the dream she'd just had.

She reached for the coffee beans, scooped out five table-spoons, and dumped them into the grinder.

The network producer was an enigma. He was wealthy. He was powerful, at least in his little niche of the industry. He was talented. Building Taste Network from nothing to a top contender in the ratings race was evidence of that.

And he was intensely disliked.

The coffee grinder whirred as Kate ground the beans.

Plenty of people were angry with him, perhaps wanted him out of their lives.

She poured the coffee into the filter.

What was she missing?

As she poured water into the coffeemaker, she pondered the dream that had faded too quickly.

She had just pressed the start button on the machine when the dream came back to her. The yellow Hummer ... driving along the creek bank, along the same path where Precious McFie's ghost was said to roam. In her dream, the ghost, dressed in white lace, opened the vehicle's door and lured Newt Keller out. He left the Hummer willingly, and then they danced along the path, the same path that led back to the Hamilton Springs Hotel. Just as Kate was about to see the bride's face, the ghostly figure melted into the ground like the Wicked Witch of the West.

Kate shook off the dream, filled her coffee mug, and started for the living room. Midstep, she halted.

What if Newt Keller was romantically involved with someone? She was so accustomed to thinking of him as intensely disliked that she found it hard to believe someone might actually enjoy his company, perhaps even love him.

But enough musing for now, she decided. Her brain was beginning to hurt and it wasn't yet dawn.

She sat down in her rocking chair, reached for her Bible on the lamp table, and flipped it open to the Psalms. Her gaze fell on Psalm 31:24—*Be strong and courageous, all you who put your hope in the Lord!*

Oh, Lord, she breathed. *How I need your strength this day; how I need your wisdom, your grace, your joy . . . How we all do! I lift my friend Susannah before you and ask that you would strengthen her heart. Wrap her in your peace. Strengthen her heart . . .*

DAWN WAS JUST BREAKING when Kate sat down in front of the computer, flipped it on, and waited while it loaded its myriad programs.

After a half-dozen minutes and an equal number of sips of coffee, the search-engine screen was up and running.

She typed in "Newt Keller." Several minutes later, a list appeared. Taste Network was at the top. She clicked on the link, then scrolled through the menu, reading in greater detail about the three celebrity chefs who had come with him to Copper Mill, as well as the nine other chefs who completed the network lineup. Next, she worked her way through other employees in the network, studying their photos and bios.

She'd read through most of the names when one caught her attention: Jacqueline Keller. Her photograph was next to her name. The name couldn't be a coincidence. Was Jacqueline Newt's wife? If so, Taste Network was a family-run business, because Jacqueline was the chief financial officer. And she looked about as friendly as Newt Keller. Or Attila the Hun.

Kate made a mental note to ask Susannah about the relationship.

Next on the list were magazine articles and newspaper accounts of Newt's activities at the network. At the bottom of the search page were accounts of his presence at social events. Thinking she might find out about the relationship to Jacqueline, Kate clicked on the first of the links.

The initial account was from several years before and told her nothing. Next came a more recent event, and Newt's name was mentioned in passing. But nothing on Jacqueline.

Then she clicked on an article from an industry-awards dinner. It took several minutes for the Web-site content to load. Kate sat back with her coffee and waited.

The first photograph appeared, then the second ... interminably slow. Third ... Fourth ... Finally the fifth photo appeared.

Kate almost spit out her coffee. She sat forward, gaping at the screen. There, dressed to kill, were Newt Keller and Nicolette Pascal.

Newt's arm was snugly fixed around Nicolette's waist, and they were gazing at each other with adoration. Romantic adoration. Love.

KATE ARRIVED AT MONDAY morning's taping just before nine. She was walking across the foyer toward the studio when Sybil Hudson called out to her.

She turned as the hotel manager zigzagged through knots of Copper Mill Tasties and Taste Network crew members.

"I was hoping to catch you before you went in," Sybil said. "There's been another sighting."

"The ghost?"

She nodded. "Sometime after midnight last night. This time it was worse than ever. A guest says this apparition appeared out of nowhere and pushed him down the stairs."

"Oh no," Kate said. "That can't be."

"He saw the . . . thing. Described it exactly as others have."

Renee stepped up from somewhere behind Kate. "Your guest probably had a little too much bubbly, if you know what I mean. You'll need to get evidence in case he brings charges. Saw the same thing once on *CSI*."

Sybil fixed a stare on Renee. Kate knew the look. She'd used it with her kids when they were little. It was a look that said, "I've got one nerve left, and you're stepping on it."

Renee didn't pick up on The Look. She opened her mouth to say more but halted when her mother called to her from the other side of the foyer. "Kisses is acting funny again," Caroline said. "You better get over here."

"I'll come back tonight," Kate told Sybil as Renee started to walk away. "We've got to get to the bottom of this."

"I'll be here. This has gone on long enough." She paused. "The guest said something that makes me think this-haunting is real. He described the same frigid wind I've felt when I've looked around after someone has reported a sighting."

"Was the man hurt?"

"Not physically. But Renee's right. Now he's saying he might sue us for the emotional trauma he experienced."

From the corner of her eye, Kate saw Kisses crouching and growling. His little ears flopped as he followed something that was invisible to the human eye, just as he had in the parking lot the night the apparition floated in front of the hotel windows.

Kate shivered.

A FEW MINUTES LATER, Kate took her seat in the studio audience. This was to be Susannah's final episode, and Kate knew how badly she wanted it to go well.

But things started out rocky from the beginning. Daryl briefly lost her sunny disposition when she found out Susannah had switched from tiramisu to a quadruple-chocolate-fudge cake.

"I can't believe you did this without consulting me," Kate heard Daryl say. "We're on a tight schedule, and you can't just snap your fingers and expect the new ingredients, utensils, and bakeware to magically appear." Her bouncy, smiling persona was still intact, but something else had crept in beside it. Something that said in no uncertain terms that she was stepping into Newt's position. She had taken charge.

"No need to worry," Susannah said evenly. "I came down here early this morning to make whatever shifts were necessary. Everything is taken care of. I've wanted to try out this new recipe for some time now. It will work, believe me."

Daryl let out an audible sigh. "But why did you make the switch? The tiramisu would have been a much better visual.

And it's in your next book, right? I thought you wanted to pro-
mote the book, and that was one of the reasons—"

Susannah held up a hand. "We'll do that another time.
This works better for now, let's just say because of personal
reasons and let it go at that."

Even from the distance between them, Kate could see
Susannah's cheeks redden.

Daryl shook her head slowly, then hurried off, clipboard
in hand, consulting with the soundman and camera crew. As
soon as the makeup artist was finished with Susannah, she
came out to stand in front of the studio audience.

The audience clapped and cheered.

With a grin, she held up a hand. "Hey, dear ones, we're
not through yet but thank you for the vote of confidence."
She hesitated and took a few steps closer. "No matter how
this segment turns out, and I'm hoping it will be wonderful—
actually, make that I'm *expecting* it to be wonderful—I want
to thank you for being such a great audience."

Everyone cheered again. Susannah bowed and blew them
kisses. "As a special thank-you," she said, "watch your mail-
boxes. I'll be sending everyone a copy of *Chocolates to Die For*
as soon as it releases."

"Wahoo!" Caroline shouted from behind Kate.

"Mama, you don't even cook," Renee said.

"I just love free stuff," Caroline said.

As usual, Susannah revved up her charming humor once
the cameras started rolling. Kate sat back with tears in her
eyes. One would never know her friend had a care in the world.
She became the Susannah of old, dancing around the kitchen,
cracking jokes, and mugging for the camera. The decades

rolled away as Kate remembered how she and Susannah had spent so much time in Kate's family kitchen.

Halfway through the taping, Armand Platt emerged from the Bristol kitchen to join Susannah. His humor meshed with hers as if they'd been partners in the kitchen for years.

"Honey, when you're through with your internship here at the Bristol," she said to him at the end of the show, "you come see me."

Susannah looked straight into the camera and winked. "You heard it here first, folks. And don't we make a great team?"

The audience cheered as Susannah's upbeat signature music began to play. Susannah and Armand bowed to each other and then to the audience.

"Remember," Susannah said to the camera with a wide smile, "from all of us at Sumptuous Chocolates, good-bye and God bless." Then with a wink, she said, "Until we eat again!"

After the show, Kate hurried to Susannah's side. "A tour de force, even after the difficult switch."

Susannah shrugged. "I couldn't do the tiramisu, not after Nicolette's accusation."

Daryl was talking to the cameraman nearest them but glanced up when she heard Nicolette mentioned. A moment later, she came over. "What accusation was that?"

"It's a private matter," Susannah said.

"I'm director of this show, and anything that affects the quality of the taping is my business. You made a last-minute switch that brought the show down a notch. That makes it my business."

Just then, Nicolette came through the door leading from the foyer to the temporary studio. Strangely, a cold wind seemed to blow through the door with her. Kate watched Nicolette cross the distance to the stage, then stop and stare at Susannah. Cold wind? That might have been her imagination. Cold-hearted demeanor? Judging by the look on Nicolette's face, Kate decided that, at least, wasn't her imagination.

Susannah glanced at Nicolette, then back to Daryl. "Ask your mother, honey. I'm sure she'll be happy to tell you."

As Susannah and Kate walked to the foyer, Kate told her about the Internet search she had done that morning.

"Who is Jacqueline Keller?" Kate asked. "I pulled up the Web site for Taste Network and was surprised to see someone with the Keller name as CFO."

"She's Newt Keller's ex-wife. They've been divorced for five years or so, but he still has to answer to her. She holds the purse strings."

"Does she have much say-so in the everyday running of the business?"

"Not a lot, but when ratings are down, she gets agitated and becomes very hands-on. Newt can be a bear to work with, but she makes him look like an angel."

Kate chuckled. "It sounds like they deserved each other."

Susannah laughed with her. "She keeps him on a pretty tight financial leash. She figures she was a partner with him in the Taste Network start-up, and she wants every bit of the revenue it generates now."

"Quite a divorce settlement."

Susannah nodded. "It was before my time, but it's still talked about when ratings start to slip."

"Are they slipping now?"

"It's hard to tell. They were soaring just a few months ago, but Newt's lost some good chefs because of how he treated them. Ratings dipped as a result. He's made no bones about the reason he chose the Hamilton Springs for an off-site show."

"The ghost. Which makes for intrigue—and publicity."

"Exactly."

"What about any romantic alliance—with someone else, I mean? Is the former Mrs. Keller the jealous type?"

Susannah thought for a minute. "I wouldn't say so, but there have been rumors . . ."

"Of him being romantically involved with someone?"

"No, nothing like that. Of Jacqueline stalking him."

Kate's eyebrow shot up. "You're kidding."

"Not at all. But it has more to do with how he spends his money than anything else. Seems it's become an obsession with her. Rumor has it that she's followed him to car dealerships, clothing stores, jewelers, that sort of thing."

"Is it public record? I mean, he didn't have to get a court order to stop her, did he?"

"Not that I know of. As I said, it's a rumor. It's possible he's made false accusations against her. I don't know anyone who's actually witnessed Jacqueline stalking him."

Kate let the new information sink in. "Do you see her as someone who might act on her annoyance, or even anger, with him?"

"The Hummer is new, and that might have caused her some grief. But honestly, though it was expensive, I can't imagine she would try to do him in over something like that."

Do him in? Kate thought about that for a minute. For some

reason, she kept returning to the idea that he was abducted, not worse. "I saw a photograph of Newt with Nicolette. It was taken at an awards ceremony. They looked very chummy."

"I know they've dated, but I don't know if it's anything more than that."

Kate and Susannah hugged good-bye, then Kate watched her friend head toward the stairs to return to her room. The slope of her shoulders told the real story. The worry of what was to come with the investigation seemed to be weighing heavily on her.

And the new information about Newt and his ex-wife added complicated new dots to those Kate was already trying to connect . . . but getting nowhere.

She turned toward the hotel exit but sensed that someone was watching her. Before reaching for the door, she glanced toward the doorway leading to the Taste studio.

Nicolette Pascal, head tilted back slightly, gave her a slight smile and toodled a wave with her fingers.

But that wasn't what made Kate shudder. It was the cold, calculating look in her eyes. A look of warning. And with it, the same frigid breeze she felt earlier.

She met Nicolette's unblinking gaze for just an instant. Then the corner of Nicolette's mouth quirked into a mysterious half smile. And with a graceful twirl of her skirt, she crossed the foyer with the confidence of a runway model, high heels tapping across the polished wood floors.

Chapter Thirteen

Pirates, that's what!" Renee narrowed her eyes as she peered into the dark night toward the creek. "Modern-day pirates. I saw something similar on *CSI*. No ghosts at all; that's why the boat is there. The question now is, what are they stealing and why?"

Renee trotted between Kate and Sybil as they headed from the hotel along the path leading to the creek. Her new army-surplus night-vision binoculars swung from a strap around her neck, and her small camera was at the ready. Kisses growled from his carrier, a backpack she wore slung over one shoulder.

Kate hadn't expected to see Renee when she arrived to hold vigil with Sybil, but apparently Renee had overheard Kate tell Sybil she would be out to investigate the ghost that night.

Sybil stopped and gave Renee another of her annoyed looks. "A pirate wouldn't have pushed my guest down the stairs last night. I doubt that pirates—modern or not—have anything to do with this."

"The rowboat's significant, believe you me," Renee said with equal annoyance in her expression. "And you might want to see if anything in the hotel is missing. China from the Bristol, silver service—"

"Shh," Kate whispered. "Listen!"

The faintest sound came from the direction of the hotel, and the three women turned to look.

It was the sound of a sudden wind. Shutters banged, and tree limbs bent with the force of it. It was as if the wind's source was somewhere in the hotel . . . but that was impossible.

The hair on the back of Kate's neck stood on end.

The sound whistled and whirled, then just as quickly as it started, it died down.

"Oh my," Sybil said, her voice shaking.

"I doubt that pirates could do that," Renee breathed, the tremor in her voice even more pronounced than Sybil's.

Kate swallowed hard. "I'm going in—"

But before she could finish, the parking-lot lights blinked off and on, then off again. The lights in the hotel did the same. From inside his carrier, Kisses growled ominously.

"Oh dear," breathed Renee, turning in a slow circle. "Look at that, would you? The lights in town . . ."

Kate followed her gaze and gasped. ". . . are off," she finished. "I wonder if the whole town is without power." She started to dial Paul on her cell but had punched in only three numbers when, behind her, Sybil uttered a little cry.

She turned back toward the hotel, almost afraid to look.

There, on the second floor, just as before, a ghostly figure seemed to float behind flickering candlelight. This time, it was clear the figure was female, and she wore a wedding gown and veil.

Kate's heart pounded against her ribs, and she caught her breath. "I . . . I don't believe in such things," she said to the others, mustering her courage. "I'm going to march right up there this minute. Anyone who wants to can come along."

Renee and Sybil exchanged worried glances, then Renee shrugged. "I'm in."

"I hate to admit it, but I don't want to stay out here in the dark alone," Sybil said.

On their way to the entrance, Kate called Paul, who confirmed that the power had gone out at their house as well. At the same time, Renee called her mother, who said the lights had flickered and gone out at their home.

"Nothing in here," Kate whispered several minutes later, aiming the beam of her penlight into the first of the three rooms where the ghost had appeared, the room nearest the laundry room.

Sybil and Renee then followed her to the next room.

"Nor here," she said after giving the room a cursory scan with the light.

Then they stepped into the third room, the room with all the tables and chairs, and looked in, following the beam of Kate's penlight. Nothing seemed to have been disturbed since the first time Kate examined the room. Renee and Sybil returned to the hallway, which still held the odd chill Sybil described earlier.

Kate reached for the door handle, then as she swung the beam around for one last look, she spotted a mark on the conference table.

She moved closer. The table was just dusty enough to show a hint of a footprint. The print was small, probably made by a woman, and the imprint was only of the toe of a shoe. She had seen the imprint before. It was made by a ballet slipper.

The other women returned to the room and peered over her shoulder. They stared at the footprint for a moment, then Renee reached for her camera and snapped a picture. She sniffed when the other two gave her a quizzical look, and said, "It will come in handy for the investigation."

"Room 213," Kate said, looking down the hallway a moment later. "Newt Keller's room?"

Sybil looked embarrassed and didn't answer right away. Finally, she nodded and said, "Yes. The reporter was right. That's his room."

"Why did the reservations people put him here? I thought these were unused rooms." Kate took a few steps closer to the closed door and fixed her penlight beam on the room number. "It's the room Precious McFie died in, and this wing of the hotel is thought to be haunted by her ghost. Yet you still assigned him room 213?"

"He requested it," Sybil said quietly.

Kate blinked. "He requested it?"

"And he asked me to keep his room number confidential. When a guest makes that kind of a request, I honor it. That's why I didn't tell you before."

Renee frowned, staring at the door. "Maybe he's into séances. I saw that once on a *Law and Order* episode. Turned out to be a setup. The perp just did it to get rid of—"

"Wait!" Kate held a finger to her lips. "Do you hear that?"

Kisses growled from inside his carrier, then whined and growled again as a shutter banged against a wall outside the room with the footprint.

"The wind," Kate whispered. "It's back."

Just then the lights flickered, buzzed, then stayed on. Kate put her shoulders back and smiled. "A simple power outage, that's all." Her knees obviously didn't get the message. They had turned to jelly again.

Chapter Fourteen

Strange about the power outage last night," Paul said over their morning coffee. "Sam said it was out at his place too."

"That doesn't seem so strange," Kate said, leaning back and holding a warm mug between both hands. "If a car hit a power pole or some such thing, the blackout would have been localized."

"Sam said he heard the power company can't determine the cause. It's also odd that the entire grid wasn't involved—which normally would be the case."

"Grid?"

"It has to do with a big maplike board the power-company dispatchers use to route electricity through the region. Certain areas are linked together in sections called grids. This outage happened without involving the entire grid for our area."

Kate took a sip of coffee. "I refuse to believe the lights went out because of ghost activity."

Paul laughed. "I agree, but it is bizarre."

"I know I keep saying this, but there's got to be a logical explanation for these weird occurrences." She took another sip of coffee, then put down her mug. "Plus I have the uncanny feeling that Newt Keller's disappearance and Precious McFie's appearance are connected somehow." She stood to get the coffeemaker carafe and refill their mugs. "I just can't connect the dots."

She sat down again, and Paul put his hand over hers. "I worry about you getting so involved with this. And I worry you're not getting the rest you need. You're up and at it early every morning, off to the tapings or to sleuth. Sometimes both."

"It's Susannah," she said. "I can't stop until I find the real suspect." She leaned forward. "Paul, she may be arrested. . . ."

He frowned. "Has the investigation gone that far?"

"I don't think so, but Sheriff Roberts did tell her not to leave town. It was quite a blow. She had intended to leave right after the shoot was done." She studied Paul's face, almost as if the answers might be written in his eyes. "If she's arrested, Paul . . ."

"For a while you thought she might be guilty."

"It hurts me to say this, but the jury is still out. She seems to be holding things back, which troubles me. On the other hand, I've been around her for a week, seen her in all kinds of interactions—both good and bad—and I can't imagine she could have done anything to harm Newt Keller. It's just not in her, Paul." She paused and took another sip of coffee.

Paul grinned. "Do I see a look in your eye that says you may be onto something?"

"Not really—at least, nothing concrete. Just that smattering of unconnected dots, maybe some possible theories, some people around her who seem ready to set her up, then there's the research I've done online . . ." She ruffled Paul's hair, then leaned over to kiss his cheek. "All this means I've got to dig deeper to get to the truth. It also means I won't rest until I find out the truth."

Paul quirked a brow. "Ah, more cookies?"

She ruffled his hair again. "Sorry, big guy, not this time. It means I'm off to the *Chronicle* office to do more sleuthing."

"The *Chronicle*?"

"Or, as the town paper was known many years ago, the *Copper Mill Bugle*."

KATE ARRIVED AT THE NEWSPAPER OFFICE just before ten. A low, rhythmic rumble echoed across the hillside just as she exited the Honda. It was distant at first, then grew louder. Kate looked up.

A helicopter appeared from behind a bank of clouds in the west, circled the town about a thousand feet off the ground, then headed northeast along the creek. It was obviously part of a search effort for Newt Keller. The chopper whipped its way along, hovering for minutes at a time before moving forward again.

Kate watched it for a few minutes before reaching the entrance to the *Chronicle* building. Just as she did, her cell phone buzzed. She stepped to one side of the door and flipped her phone open.

"Kate," breathed Renee. "Did you hear the chopper?"

Kate couldn't help smiling. When *CSI* or *Law and Order* weren't on, Renee probably watched *MASH* reruns.

"I did. It just flew over the *Chronicle* office."

"Rattled the dishes here," Renee said. "Mama almost dove under the table." She dropped her voice. "But that's not why I called. I just talked to my neighbor Lola. . . ."

Renee's personal grapevine was alive and well. Kate smiled as she waited to hear what Lola had heard from her sister, who heard it from Skip Spencer's mother, who heard it from Deputy Spencer—the usual order of communication in Renee's gossip circle.

"Apparently Newt Keller has an ex-wife who's a bigwig in the network hierarchy. At least that's what Skip Spencer's mother said. And the chopper's her doing. In fact, she may even be in it."

"She's taking part in the search?"

"More like she's taken *over* the search. She insisted the investigation be revved up. Apparently, she said she was going to call the governor if Sheriff Roberts didn't get the FBI involved. So, according to Skip Spencer, who told his mother, who told Lola's sister . . ."

Kate bit her tongue and prayed for the grace not to interrupt.

". . . the sheriff called Ms. Keller's bluff. He said he didn't need some hoity-toity civilian from Nashville telling him how to run his investigation. And, honestly, I don't blame him. Anyhow, she ended up calling the governor, who, it turns out, went to high school with Ms. Keller. The governor then called in the FBI, and now Sheriff Roberts is fit to be tied. FBI agents are about to swarm into town and take over the investigation. Ms. Keller is on her way. Like I said, that might have been her in the chopper."

Renee stopped and audibly caught her breath. Kate felt out of breath just from listening.

"Why did she wait so long?" It had been several days since Newt Keller disappeared. Kate found it odd that, if she were that concerned, she hadn't jumped in from the beginning.

"Apparently she was touring the South of France. One of those wine and gourmet-food tasting deals. Took some time for the news to reach her, Lola said, then even longer to get a flight back to the States."

Kate heard whining and yipping in the background.

"Must run," Renee said. "I need to cook up a meal for Little Umpkins."

Pondering what she'd just heard, and nearly frozen from standing out in the cold, Kate reached for the office door.

Her cell phone buzzed again. When she flipped it open, Renee said, "I nearly forgot to tell you. The word is Sheriff Roberts is being pressured by the governor to make an arrest."

Kate's heart caught. "Oh dear."

"My words exactly. Skip's mother couldn't—or wouldn't—name the prime suspect. But Skip said there definitely is one. I've seen many cases where the authorities arrest someone because of political pressure."

That the cases Renee was talking about were on TV shows didn't matter. Kate knew it was true.

The helicopter did another circle around town. "I'm sorry. I can't hear you," Kate shouted into the phone.

Renee obviously couldn't hear Kate either, because after a few seconds, she hung up.

Kate watched the helicopter head northeast again, this time on a route keeping it a mile or so from Copper Mill Creek.

It disappeared over some rolling hills, and as the throbbing beat of the blades echoed across the valley, all she could think was that her dear childhood friend was about to be arrested.

Chapter Fifteen

Kate wanted nothing more than to drive to the hotel to be with Susannah. But she told herself she could do more good sleuthing around to find the real culprit in Newt Keller's disappearance and clear Susannah's name once and for all.

So, bracing herself for a few more minutes in the cold, she called her friend instead.

Susannah picked up on the first ring. She sounded relieved to hear from Kate, but there was also deep worry in her normally ebullient tone.

"I feel like a criminal, but I didn't do anything wrong."

"I'm doing my best to figure all this out, Suse." She imagined her friend's smile at the sound of her childhood name.

"Can you tell me what you've found?" The hope in her voice was heartrending.

"Not yet," Kate said. "And most of it is theory, anyway. I'm at the newspaper office to check on some old accounts of the Hamilton Springs ghost."

There was a moment of dead silence, then Susannah said, "What does that have to do with Newt Keller's disappearance?"

"I may be jumping off a gangplank in my thinking, but something tells me the hauntings might be connected to Newt's disappearance."

"Gangplank?" Susannah chuckled at last.

Kate laughed with her. "I'll stop by later."

"I'd like nothing better," Susannah said. "You'll notice when you drive in that there's an agent posted at the front door."

"What in the world for?"

"I'm assuming it's to make sure I don't escape." She laughed. "So maybe you'd better not bring the file in the cake after all."

Moments after ending the call, Kate let herself in the front door of the newspaper office. The *Chronicle* building was a decades-old house that had been converted into offices. The room that served both as foyer and reception area had a river-rock fireplace, and on that chilly morning, a fire crackled and popped.

Down a central hall, Kate could see the smaller offices of Jennifer McCarthy, who did most of the reporting, and Lucy Mae Briddle was at the front desk.

Lucy Mae looked up and smiled as Kate approached the front desk. "Kate, it's good to see you."

"It's good to see you too," Kate said. "I read your article about the high-school band concert last week. It was wonderfully written; I could almost see the wave of the music-teacher's baton and hear that trombone solo."

"Well, thank you." Lucy Mae's smile widened. Her hair was dark with a few streaks of gray, and she wore it in a feminine but no-nonsense short style. Her most striking feature was the color of her eyes—a lustrous gray—under perfectly shaped eyebrows. Silver hoop earrings graced her ears.

"What can I do for you, Kate?"

"I'm doing some research on the alleged haunting at the Hamilton Springs Hotel."

"Ah yes, the Precious McFie case."

"That's the one."

Lucy Mae nodded. "It's truly been the buzz around town since the Joel St. Nicklaus book was published. We're running an ad for his book as well as the signing at the library. Will you and Pastor Hanlon be attending?"

"We haven't decided yet, but I would like to hear what the author has to say about his research."

Lucy Mae picked up a notepad and pencil. "Speaking of research, how can we help with the McFie story?"

"I checked the library, and their microfiche collection doesn't go back far enough. I'm looking for local accounts of her death."

"You realize the *Chronicle* wasn't in existence at that time."

"Yes, but I understand that the *Copper Mill Bugle* was very much alive and well. I'm hoping some enterprising reporter covered the tragic circumstances of her death." She sighed. "Honestly, I'm looking for anything that will give me a glimpse into the young girl's life and provide some background for what's going on now."

Lucy Mae frowned. "The *Bugle* was printed on a single sheet of paper, maybe fifteen inches wide and yea tall." She blocked off a rough measurement of about two feet with her hands. "Several years ago at the Copper Mill centennial celebration, someone found some of the old editions up in the attic and made copies to sell. Because our offices are located in what was once a home, and the home was originally owned by the publisher of the *Bugle*, the attic has been a treasure trove of resources from the past."

Kate leaned forward. "Did those old editions contain anything about the Hamilton Springs Hotel, or as it was known back then, the Copper Creek Hotel? Or Precious McFie?"

"To be honest, I have no idea. But I'll be happy to pull them out for you. Those that were found for the centennial celebration are stored in one of the back offices. Getting to the rest takes a little more courage."

"Courage?"

She raised an eyebrow and grinned. "Follow me."

They went up a flight of stairs and started down a hall. Halfway down the hall, Lucy Mae stopped and looked up at the ceiling, where the attic stairs were concealed. A cord with a wooden spool hung down from one end of the pull-down lid.

Kate gaped. "Up there?"

"That's the place. It's dusty, musty, and covered with spiderwebs. We avoid it at all costs."

At the thought of spiderwebs, Kate squirmed. "Still, if it's the treasure trove you say it is, I really would like to take a look." She glanced at her watch. Paul wasn't expecting her home for lunch, and she had until four to meet Susannah. "Just give me a broom and a flashlight. You won't even know I'm there."

"And some bug spray," said a voice from behind her.

Kate turned. Jennifer McCarthy had come out of her office and was leaning against the wall, arms crossed. "You must really want to take a look at those old *Bugles*."

"It's a long shot," Kate admitted. "But I've got to get to the bottom of this haunted-hotel business."

"You think it's connected to Keller's disappearance?"

"Don't quote me, but it's gone through my mind."

Jennifer nodded but didn't comment. "If you discover something, could you let us know?"

"Of course."

Jennifer walked closer. "More media poured into town this morning—all big city or national. Hard to elbow my way in for any interviews."

"If this turns out as I'm hoping it will, I promise I'll try to get my friend Susannah Applebaum to grant you an exclusive."

"I hear she's the top suspect based on circumstantial evidence," Jennifer said. "Can you give a comment on that at this time?"

"No, it's too early."

Kate looked up at the attic opening, then back to Lucy Mae.

"Well?" she said with a grin. "Lead me to your broom, a flashlight, and bug spray."

Ten minutes later, Kate sat down in the dim light of the attic window and glanced nervously about for crawling critters. She'd swept a small area free of cobwebs, then sprayed the perimeter with insect repellent. Soon she was flipping through storage boxes of old newspapers. Many were brittle and musty, and several editions were stuck together from years of moisture.

It was past noon when Kate paused to glance at her watch. Her head was aching from eye strain, and her stomach was complaining that it had been too long since breakfast.

She gazed at the stacks of papers and boxes, feeling disappointment setting in. She had pinned high hopes on this search, even though she didn't really know what she was looking for.

She had one box to go. Ignoring the ache that was radiating from the small of her back down her right leg, she pulled the box over to the window, lifted the lid, and peered into its musty depths.

Then she saw the date on the file, and her breath caught. "Oh my," she whispered, then shouted, "Oh my!" She pulled out the November 22, 1929, special edition of the *Bugle* and held it up to the beam of her flashlight.

Thirty seconds later, Jennifer and Lucy Mae clambered up the stairs, obviously responding to her triumphant shout. Kate smiled to herself. Journalistic curiosity had taken precedence over their aversion to spiders, cobwebs, and dust. She gave them a triumphant grin as they entered the attic and stooped to avoid hitting their heads on the open beams. "I've found just what I needed! But you have to promise me you won't publish anything about it until I flush out our prime suspect—and believe me, it isn't Susannah Applebaum."

Jennifer exchanged glances with Lucy Mae, then nodded. "Not a difficult promise. We're a weekly, remember?"

Ten minutes later, Kate opened the door of her Honda, scooted in, and put the key in the ignition. She was dusty, grimy, and kept imagining she felt a stray cobweb—or worse, the maker of the cobweb—brushing against her face. Even so, she couldn't stop smiling as she drove home.

Her cell phone rang just as she walked into the kitchen. She checked the caller ID. It was Susannah.

"Wait till you hear what I found out," Kate said, dropping her handbag on the counter.

Susannah's voice was somber, and she sounded scared. "It will have to wait, Katie. I'm afraid I need to cancel our tea."

"Oh dear. I'm sorry—"

"I'm being taken in for more questioning, this time by the FBI."

"Oh no!" Kate's heart skipped a beat, and she sank into a chair. "I'll be right there; I'll go with you."

"Thanks for the offer, but I'm sure they wouldn't let you stay with me during the questioning. I'll call as soon as he's finished. I just hope it won't take long."

She paused, and when she continued, her voice was stronger. "The Bible verse Paul read last Sunday keeps going through my mind. It's all that's bolstering my courage right now. *'When you go through deep waters and great trouble, I will be with you.'* I keep repeating those last five words, and somehow, Kate, they're giving me strength."

Chapter Sixteen

Livvy called that afternoon and asked Kate if she could stop by and vent after she left the library. When Kate opened the front door, Livvy grinned at her from beneath her parka's faux-fur hood.

Kate quickly invited her in out of the cold.

"I heard we might get snow later tonight," Livvy said as she warmed her hands by the fire.

"It feels like snow," Kate said. "I just hope our guys are home before the storm sets in."

Paul and Danny were at the church for an emergency board meeting about the ghost issue—instigated by Renee Lambert.

"How about some coffee or tea?" Kate asked.

"Tea sounds great."

Livvy slipped off her coat. Kate took it with her on the way to the kitchen and hung it on the coat tree in the entry.

Kate put on the teakettle, then returned to the living room. She stoked the fire and closed the screen, then sat down at the opposite end of the sofa from Livvy, curling her legs beneath her. They chatted for a bit about the latest developments—Susannah being taken in for questioning, the involvement of the FBI and Newt's ex-wife, the photo of Newt and Nicolette, and the discoveries Kate had made at the *Chronicle* office.

Livvy's eyes narrowed when Kate told her that she was still puzzling over the pocket knife she'd found jammed into the Hummer's CD player.

"What significance do you think it has?"

"I'm still not sure. It doesn't make sense. If it's the weapon the abductor used to force Newt out of the vehicle, why would he—or she—tuck it into the CD?"

"To get rid of it in a hurry?" Livvy suggested.

"If the perpetrator wanted to do that, he or she would maybe put it in a pocket or maybe throw it into the creek." Kate paused. "I'm thinking the only one who would want to hang onto it would be Newt himself."

Livvy leaned forward. "You mean there's a scuffle, he gets the knife back, then hides it in the CD player? Why would he do that?"

"Maybe he wanted to leave a clue," Kate said quietly, then shrugged.

"This is a complicated case." She shook her head slowly.

Kate treasured Livvy's input when she was puzzling out a mystery—or, as in this case, two or three mysteries, strangely intertwined. But that evening, Livvy seemed distracted.

Kate suddenly felt sorry she had spent so much time talking about the case. She touched Livvy's hand. "It's your turn," she said. "You said you needed to vent."

"After hearing about Susannah, I hate to bring up my worries," Livvy said. "They seem trivial in comparison. But the truth is, I'm about ready to tear out my hair." As if on cue, she tucked a strand of auburn hair behind her ear.

Kate raised an eyebrow. "The book signing?"

Livvy nodded.

"It's gotten that bad?"

"Remember how I worried this whole thing would become a circus?"

"It's hit the three-ring stage?"

"Clowns and all." Livvy laughed lightly, shaking her head. "Only they're dressed like ghosts. I'm trying to get things to calm down before Joel St. Nicklaus arrives. Maybe I'm expecting too much, but I'd rather Copper Mill put forward a more sophisticated front. Instead, we've got the Caspers and the Ghostbusters holding their respective signs." She shook her head. "Lucy Mae Briddle heard about it and stopped by to interview people on both sides. I'm sure the article will be in Thursday's paper, complete with photos."

The teakettle sang out, and Kate hurried to the kitchen to pour their tea. She soon returned with a small tray that held their cups of tea, a sugar bowl, teaspoons, and a small plate of brownies. She placed the tray on the coffee table and handed Livvy a teacup and saucer. She took the other cup for herself. They each took a brownie from the small plate on the tray.

She sat down again, facing Livvy, and sipped her tea thoughtfully. "Paul and I have been talking about this a lot. About the possibility of ghosts, I mean."

"From a spiritual, or biblical, perspective, you mean?"

Kate nodded. "Some people believe there's a real world of spirits, and that it's completely scriptural. Others don't.

Still others are confused and don't know what they believe. That may be why local pastors are getting so many calls about this."

Livvy sighed. "Just one of many things in the Bible we can't understand now, but will someday."

"Now we see things imperfectly as in a cloudy mirror, but then we will see everything with perfect clarity," Kate quoted.

"That verse has always been a comfort to me," Livvy said. "There's so much we don't—and can't—understand." She took a sip of her tea. "Are you and Paul going to come to the signing?"

"We don't want to do anything to fan the flames. It's our intent to remain neutral."

Livvy quirked a brow and gave Kate a half smile. "I bet I can get you to change your mind."

"What have you got up your sleeve?"

"Remember the professional storyteller I mentioned?"

Kate nodded.

"You'll never guess who she is." Livvy took another sip of tea and watched Kate over the rim of her teacup. "Give up?"

"I can't imagine . . ." Then a light began to dawn. What would be the one story that would make her change her mind? She grinned. "Wait, don't tell me. It's someone who's going to tell the story of Precious McFie?"

"Better than that. A grandniece of Precious McFie herself. It just so happens she's a professional storyteller, and this story is part of her repertoire."

"Oh my!" Kate's hand flew to her mouth. "You're right. I wouldn't miss this for the world."

IT WAS STILL DARK when Kate awoke. She quickly swung her legs out of bed and grabbed her robe. A light snow had begun falling the previous night when she and Paul had turned out the lights and gone to bed. There was something about a fresh snow that made her feel like a little girl on Christmas morning—she couldn't wait to get up and have a look before it began to melt.

That morning was no different. She went straight to the living room and opened the drapes. The sight that greeted her made her catch her breath. A thin powdered-sugar coating of snow covered the backyard, outlining every tree branch and shrub.

The sky was turning a pearl gray, creating just enough light to give the snowy landscape the look of a fairyland. A bright red cardinal landed on the maple just outside the window and hopped onto the birdfeeder. He was soon followed by another cardinal and then a titmouse and a handful of sparrows. Their fluttering caused the powdery snow to spill from the branches above them as if from a flour sifter.

In spite of her worries about Susannah and the mysteries she was having trouble solving, the beauty of the morning lifted Kate's heart.

Sometimes God gave her little gifts like this to remind her that he was still in charge. Who else but the Creator could create such artistry?

Lightly humming "His Eye Is on the Sparrow," she headed to the kitchen to start the coffee. Leaving it to brew, she went into the living room and flicked on the gas lighter in the fireplace. Then she gathered her Bible, her notebook, and a pen and sat down in her rocker.

She purposely pushed the myriad thoughts about the case from her mind so she could spend some much-needed time resting in God's presence. She opened her Bible to reread the passage in Isaiah that had meant so much to Susannah. As she thumbed through the pages, Isaiah 40:31 caught her eye.

Those who wait on the Lord will find new strength. They will fly high on wings like eagles. They will run and not grow weary. They will walk and not faint.

She read the passage again, thinking about Susannah and her trials. Then she bowed her head and prayed her friend would find new strength and courage in the Lord to see her through, no matter what was ahead.

Susannah had called after her questioning the night before. She sounded shaken but thankful she hadn't been charged with anything. She'd been warned again, however, not to leave Copper Mill.

Kate spent a few more minutes in the silence of early morning, covering her family and friends, Faith Briar, and the little town of Copper Mill with prayer. Then she asked for safekeeping for her day and discernment and creativity in her thinking. . . . *Creativity?* It had been a while since she'd prayed for that particular grace. She smiled and added, "Especially the latter, Lord. I need it today in abundance."

Kate drove into the hotel parking lot at a quarter to nine for Nicolette Pascal's taping. She came to an immediate halt. There wasn't a parking space to be had. Satellite dishes had sprouted like mushrooms after a soaking rain. The term *media frenzy* didn't even begin to cover the sight before her.

She sat for a moment, gaping, before swinging a U-turn and heading back out of the lot to park on the street. Directly across from the parking lot, in an empty field, sat a helicopter, its blades at rest.

A few minutes later, she twined her way through the knots of people—Taste Network cast and crew, hotel employees, curious citizenry of all ages, national and local TV and newspaper reporters, and their camera and sound crews.

She spotted Renee off to one side, near the Nicolette Pascal star coach, and headed toward her. "What's going on?"

Renee shifted her designer tote pet carrier to her other side and sidled closer to Kate, keeping her voice low. "It's a news conference," she whispered. "There's going to be an announcement."

Kate frowned. "Who called for the conference?"

"Daryl Gallagher."

Moments later, Daryl took her place at a makeshift podium in front of the hotel and asked for everyone's attention. She looked every bit the part of an up-and-coming network executive. Her bouncy demeanor was still evident, but there seemed to be a new sophistication about her. She was fitting into the new somber role with an attractive flair.

She tapped the microphone, and the hubbub around Kate subsided.

"I want to thank the citizens of Copper Mill for all you've done to help search for this man who is, as some have put it, Mr. Taste Network," she said. "We at Taste are gravely concerned. I also want to give special thanks to the cast and crew who make up the Taste family. They've carried on under the most grievous circumstances, continuing to tape the segments of the show, just as Newt himself would have done."

Slightly behind Daryl and to one side was a woman Kate

recognized as Newt's ex-wife, Jacqueline Keller. Nicolette Pascal and Birdie Birge stood on the other side. As if on cue, Jacqueline stepped forward to join Daryl at the podium.

Daryl, dressed impeccably, was poised and beautiful. She shot Jacqueline a professional smile, appropriately touched with gravitas, as if they were on the *Today* show.

Jacqueline put her arm around Daryl's shoulders. "I owe a debt of gratitude to this young woman. It was she who moved heaven and earth to find me in France and alert me to Newt's disappearance. Without her stepping forward in my absence, and because—I'm sorry to say—the local authorities were not taking Newt's abduction seriously, we would not have been able to get the professional help we needed for this search. Daryl has tirelessly kept me abreast of developments, sometimes hour by hour across the Atlantic, until I could get here myself."

Kate let her gaze drift from Jacqueline to Birdie, then to Nicolette, who was staring at Jacqueline. If looks could kill, the former Ms. Keller would have been long gone. Birdie's expression, on the other hand, was as pleasant as ever.

But Nicolette's normally cool demeanor had turned to ice.

Daryl was her daughter. Kate would have thought she would be bursting at the seams with pride, not shooting daggers at the CFO of the network that employed her.

Kate's thoughts returned to the photograph of Newt Keller and Nicolette. Of course. Kate could practically see the green-headed creature jealousy raising its head in Nicolette's heart.

After her speech, Jacqueline stepped back, and Daryl continued with the news conference, fielding questions from the media and chatting about the network, the challenges ahead, and, of course, the hope that Newt Keller would be found alive and well.

Then she took one last question.

"What about the suspect who is about to be arrested?"

"Do you mean Susannah Applebaum?"

There were gasps of surprise from the audience. Hands popped up and questions were shouted as reporters tried to get the details.

Daryl looked down, blinking as if embarrassed and ready to cry. "I'm sorry," she said after a moment, holding up both hands to stop the questions. "It was premature of me to name names. I can tell you that, yes, there is a suspect, but please consider what I just said as off the record."

Kate's cheeks flushed in distress. Until then, there had been no official statement that Susannah was a suspect. Perhaps rumors had been circulating about her possible arrest, but no one knew it as a certainty.

Off the record? Hardly. It was too juicy a tidbit for a reporter to keep to himself or herself: Susannah Applebaum, one of the three darlings of the Taste Network lineup, a suspect in her producer-director's disappearance? No, they wouldn't keep that quiet.

Daryl, regaining her composure and looking as poised as ever, drew the news conference to a close.

If Kate hadn't known better, she would have thought Daryl dropped Susannah's name on purpose.

Then again, maybe she *did* know better.

But what was her motive?

THE TAPING OF NICOLETTE'S segment was delayed because of the news conference. Kate checked her watch. She had just enough time to do a little more sleuthing on the second floor of the hotel.

She trotted into the foyer and up the left side of the large double staircase. She had only a few minutes to poke around upstairs. If her theory was right, she would find it near room 213. She rounded the corner near the hallway leading to the ghost wing. As usual, the light was dim. She blinked to let her eyes adjust and kept walking.

She heard the sounds of two women arguing, one with a distinct French accent, and the click of high heels on a wooden floor. The hallway was carpeted with a runner down its center with highly polished hardwood on either side. If someone was walking on the hardwood, simple deduction told her that two people were walking together, one on the carpet, the other on the hardwood floor.

Kate looked around quickly for a place to hide, then ducked into an alcove that appeared to have housed an *objet d'art* sometime in the past. She scrunched back as far as she could, realizing too late that she could be seen by anyone with moderate vision, even in the dim light. Not only that, her silly attempt to hide would look awfully suspicious to whoever was coming down the hall.

Better not to hide at all.

She stepped out into the hallway again. There in front of her stood two women.

"So," Nicolette said, a half smile playing at the corner of her mouth. "What brings you here?" Almost as if a sleight of hand, Nicolette slid something the size of a credit card into her pocket. It looked suspiciously like a room card key, and Kate wondered why she had it in her hand. Her room was obviously not in this wing.

Beside her, Daryl Gallagher blinked in surprise. She smiled at Kate, almost embarrassed to have startled her. But she did glance at the alcove, and a slight frown crossed her brow before the smile returned.

"We're on our way to the taping," Daryl said, still all smiles. "Are you coming?"

If Kate hadn't heard their raised voices seconds earlier, she wouldn't have known they'd been arguing.

"I wouldn't miss it," Kate said easily. "You're on today, aren't you Nicolette?"

The chef nodded curtly. "Yes, of course." She gestured to the alcove, started to speak, then apparently thought better of it and let her hand fall to her side. But a knowing smile again played at her lips.

"Mother, we need to get downstairs." Daryl glanced at her watch. "The run-through starts in just a few minutes. We can't be late. I'll never hear the end of it." She laughed lightly and cupped Nicolette's elbow with her hand as the two made their way to the end of the hall and the grand staircase beyond.

Kate listened to the fading footsteps and the click of Nicolette's heels.

The strange thing was she had seen the two women just a few minutes before at the news conference outside the hotel. How had they gotten up to that wing before she did?

What did they know that she didn't about getting around in this old hotel?

Chapter Seventeen

Fifteen minutes later, Kate entered the Taste studio and took her seat. The mother-daughter team had just begun the first run-through, and even though it was a brief rehearsal, they were putting on quite a show. Nicolette's flair in the kitchen and Daryl's directing skills were a perfect match.

The studio audience seemed enthralled with Nicolette's simple methods of French-fusion cooking, her elegant style, and of course, her charming French accent.

She began by telling the studio audience about her favorite recipe for sole meunière with a balsamic brown-butter sauce, then delighted them when she showed them how to give the dish a Southern flair by substituting catfish fillets for sole. She received a standing ovation when she presented the final product, golden brown and steaming, to the audience members who had been chosen to be the day's tasters. She chose deep-fried fingerling potatoes as a side dish, and a warm salad of collard greens sautéed in olive oil, then she finished with a sweet-and-tart apricot glaze.

Kate noticed that a few reporters had slipped in sometime before the taping started. They were just as enthusiastic as the studio audience. Surprisingly, though Daryl had asked the media to remain outside, she welcomed their participation. Lucy Mae Briddle was one of the most enthusiastic members of the press, clapping and cheering between her note taking.

During a break, Kate walked to the foyer and punched in Susannah's number on her cell. While she waited for it to ring, someone called her name.

She turned to see a woman in pink-hued designer sunglasses, a floppy-brimmed hat, a billowing caftan, and high-heeled boots headed her direction. Kate flipped the phone closed and squinted at the woman who had just called her name. She looked vaguely familiar.

It wasn't until the woman pulled off her sunglasses that recognition hit.

"Susannah!"

She grinned. "A girl has to get around without being recognized."

"Honestly, I wouldn't have known you."

She looked relieved. "Good. I've been hounded by the press and curiosity seekers a bit too long. Maybe this will keep them at bay. Katie, I have a favor to ask."

"Anything—as long as it doesn't involve killing spiders."

Susannah grinned, then gave her a quick side hug. "You haven't changed a bit." Then she sobered. "Seriously, I need to get away from here."

"And you need me to drive the getaway car?"

Susannah laughed. "Thank you for offering, but I have a

driver. I thought I'd have him move my coach over to your house. Would you mind terribly if I stayed there?"

"We'd love to have you. Can I help you move anything?"

Susannah replaced her sunglasses and shook her head. "I've already checked out of the hotel and put everything in the coach. I'm ready to roll."

They had just started toward the exit when the sound of the cheering studio audience poured from the Taste studio. Susannah stopped. "Wait, I want to see what's going on." She signaled Kate to follow, then walked over to the doorway leading to the studio.

The taping had resumed, and Nicolette was dancing around the kitchen, as graceful and light on her feet as a ballerina, bantering with the audience about the ingredients she was about to present.

She asked for a drumroll, and from the back of the stage, Armand Platt appeared and, with a grand flourish, drummed the counter with two wooden spoon handles.

After a dramatic pause, Nicolette smiled at the audience. "Tiramisu," she cried triumphantly. "And now, let me show you how to make this delicious, sumptuous dessert."

With a dramatic flutter of her fingers, she pulled out the ingredients one by one, as if they were made of pure gold. The audience sighed as she poured the orange liqueur over the ladyfingers. "Though this is usually thought of as more Italian than French," she said as she worked, "in my opinion it's decadent enough to be French."

Beside Kate, Susannah stiffened. "That's my recipe," she breathed. "I developed it specifically for *Chocolates to Die For*."

She turned to Kate. "If she goes through with this, it will be terrible. Not just for me, but for us both."

As if on cue, Nicolette halted midsentence. "Take five," she called out, scowling. "Somebody get me some coffee. And I mean right now!"

"Mother, we're right in the middle of taping . . ."

"I said I need coffee." Nicolette rubbed her forehead, her elbow on the counter. When she looked up, she spotted the women gaping at her. "Is there a problem?" she said, her French accent harsh.

Kate shook her head, but Susannah stepped forward, pulling off her sunglasses at the same time.

"Actually, there is," she said, taking a few steps farther into the studio.

"Funny, we were just talking about you, Susannah," Nicolette said with a cold smile. "Nice outfit."

"That's my recipe," Susannah said quietly. Nicolette moved toward them, slowly, deliberately, again adopting her runway model's walk.

Behind her, Daryl told the crew to take a quick break, got her mother some strong coffee, then spoke to the audience in her cheerleader's voice, but no one seemed to be listening. All eyes were on Susannah and Nicolette.

"It's obvious you got an advance copy of the book," Susannah continued, "though I don't know how you did."

"What are you talking about? This recipe has been in my family for years. I can prove it if necessary." She paused, her eyes bright with anger. "It's you, dear Susannah, who somehow lifted it from my collection."

Susannah stepped closer. "My attorney is on his way here. You'll be hearing—"

Nicolette's laugh came out in a single bitter burst. "It's a good thing you sent for him. From what I hear, he's going to be a very busy man."

"I'm telling you, Nicolette, your reputation is on the line. People will find out you got an advance copy of *Chocolates to Die For* and claimed the recipe as your own. If you don't believe it's mine, check with my publisher. I can prove how long it's been since I turned in the final manuscript."

For the first time, Nicolette looked hesitant, then her expression changed. She shook her head. "Really, Susannah, you expect me to believe all this? You're the one with the damaged reputation. I daresay, damaged beyond repair. Besides, who's going to believe someone who's the prime suspect in the disappearance of Newt Keller?" She laughed. "Think about it."

Without another word, she whirled and headed back to the taping.

"An old family recipe? The woman's heritage is French." Susannah laughed, but the sound was etched with bitterness. "Besides, there's always the missing ingredient—my secret weapon."

"Missing ingredient?" Kate raised a brow.

But Susannah didn't answer. She donned her sunglasses and murmured as if to herself, "This time Nicolette Pascal's gone too far. But she'll pay."

Her words chilled Kate to the bone. It was another threat, too similar to those Susannah had made against Newt Keller before he disappeared.

Chapter Eighteen

The coffee had just finished brewing the next morning when Kate heard a light tap at her front door. She hurried to answer it before the sound disturbed Paul.

There, in sweats and fuzzy slippers, stood Susannah. She looked rested and refreshed, and she carried a plate of fresh-baked, fragrant cinnamon rolls in her hands.

She stepped inside, glanced toward the master bedroom, then whispered, "Paul still asleep?" When Kate nodded, Susannah grinned. "Now doesn't this just remind you of old times? Next best thing to a slumber party."

"Did you make these?"

Susannah raised a brow, and Kate laughed.

"I just can't imagine your coach having a kitchen large enough to do any serious cooking or baking."

"I'll give you a tour later. But first this girl needs sustenance for the day ahead." She headed to the kitchen and placed the plateful of rolls on the counter.

"Coffee?" Without waiting for an answer, Susannah helped herself to a couple of mugs, poured the coffee, and handed a mug to Kate.

They went into the living room and sat in front of the fireplace. Outside, a songbird began to trill as the sun slanted through the branches. He was soon joined by others. Inside, the fire crackled and popped, and the fragrance of the fresh-baked cinnamon rolls blended with the aroma of fresh-brewed coffee.

Susannah's eyes filled. "I needed this, Katie. Just to get away from the awfulness of everything. My agent will be here later today with an attorney he's hired on my behalf. I may get through this without a formal arrest. But if I'm honest with myself, I have to admit that my reputation may be damaged beyond repair."

Kate leaned forward, speaking softly. "I'm no attorney, but the evidence against you is circumstantial. Plus, they haven't found Newt."

"True, but the FBI agent certainly put me through the wringer." She laughed, though the sound was hollow. "It was almost as if he wanted me to confess to something—*anything*—to get him off the hook."

Kate remembered what Renee had said about political pressure to make an arrest. She shot a little prayer heavenward that law enforcement officials would resist such pressure.

Susannah took a sip of her coffee, then said, "You started to tell me something the other day when I canceled our tea date."

Kate sat back, studying Susannah over the rim of her mug. "It may be nothing, but there's a nagging little suspicion in the back of my mind that tells me my discovery might be significant."

"I thought you were investigating the ghost sightings."

"I was, though I had this vague feeling that Newt's disappearance and the hauntings might be linked." She stood to get them refills on their coffee. "Are you ready for your cinnamon roll?"

"Do you think we should wait for Paul?" Susannah was grinning. "Or do you think we should have one now and another when he's ready for breakfast?"

Kate laughed. "What do you think my answer is?"

Susannah went with her to the kitchen, located the plates and flatware, then served up two warm and buttery frosted rolls. The years rolled away as Kate watched Susannah make herself at home in her kitchen. Tears began to form.

"What?" Susannah said when she turned around, a plate in each hand.

Kate swallowed hard before answering. "I was just thinking about my mother's kitchen, about our friendship . . . and about how hard I'm going to try to get to the bottom of all this."

"Well then, girlfriend, let's get down to business." She led the way into the living room. "I want to hear what you found out and how we can put an end to the injustice that's been meted out against me." Her words were meant to be light, but the import of their meaning stopped them both cold.

"Exactly that." Kate blinked against the watery sting in her eyes as she pressed the side of her fork into the soft roll. For a moment neither of them spoke.

When they'd finished their rolls, Kate put aside her empty plate and leaned back in her rocker. "I've inspected the upper wing of the hotel twice, always on the lookout for something that might lead me to discover the identity of the ghost.

"I found only one clue—a partial imprint of a slipper-like footprint—but it led nowhere."

She sipped her coffee, then said, "You said you have a copy of the Joel St. Nicklaus book?"

Susannah grinned. "*Famous Haunts of the South*? Yes indeedie. I know all about Precious McFie and her nighttime haunts at the Hamilton Springs Hotel. It does give one pause, I must tell you, when I'm alone in my room and turn out the light."

"I'd imagine so, especially with all the spooky activity of late."

"You've got that right." Susannah took a sip of coffee. "By the way, I love your beans. They're Kenyan, yes? French roast?"

Kate laughed. "Yes. Right on both counts. You're amazing." Then she sobered. "I searched the archives at the library and scoured old microfiche copies of the *Chronicle*, but I found nothing new about the hotel hauntings. Just the same story that's apparently been written up in *Famous Haunts*. There were references to Precious McFie's death in 1929, and the supposition that it's indeed her ghost—decked out in bridal attire—that still roams one wing of the hotel and the path along the creek."

"But you found something previously unreported?"

Kate nodded. "None of the news accounts I read at the library mentioned that Precious McFie's fiancé came back here to be with her when she died. Apparently that's as far as Joel St. Nicklaus got with his research, which is surprising for someone of his stature."

Susannah was still focused on the fiancé. "Why wouldn't that be reported?"

"The only thing I can figure is that his family was quite prominent, so the whole affair may already have been a scandal of huge proportions in that day and age. Maybe out of respect for the family, they didn't want to add any more fuel to the fire."

"Could they have thought that he killed her?"

"I wondered about that. But all the reports indicate she died of pneumonia. From the little I've gathered, I think he genuinely cared for her, even though he'd broken the engagement for another woman. He and Precious had been friends since childhood. Their families were very close."

"But the *Chronicle* reported he was here?"

"It wasn't the *Chronicle* then. The first newspaper in Copper Mill was the *Bugle*." She leaned forward. "That little one-page newspaper reported what happened in much more detail. I had to do some digging in the attic of the *Chronicle* building to find old copies of the *Bugle*."

"And . . . ?" Susannah's eyes were bright with interest.

"It seems that immediately after the break-up, Precious ran away, not telling family members where she'd gone. Somehow, she ended up in Copper Mill at the brand-new Copper Creek Hotel—what's now the Hamilton Springs Hotel. It was a destination hotel back then too, with natural hot springs and gourmet fare—a place where the rich and famous would come, knowing it was far enough away to give them the seclusion they needed.

"So Precious made her way here, bringing her wedding gown and veil, slippers, the works. She let only one person know where she was headed."

"Her former fiancé?"

"You've got it. His name was Holden Giles III. She somehow sent for him, hoping he would come back to her and they would marry here in Copper Mill without fanfare."

"Do you think he intended to marry her after all?"

"No one knows. Apparently, he didn't send word that he was on his way, so she slipped into further despair. That's when she took to walking at night along the creek in her wedding gown and veil.

"Then one night a storm blew in, covering the town with freezing rain that quickly turned to ice. According to the article, townspeople saw her walking along the creek in that wedding gown. No woolen coat or sturdy shoes or boots—not even a shawl to keep her warm. Just thin little balletlike slippers . . ."

"Ballet? Isn't that what you said you found in one of the rooms? A print like a ballet slipper?"

"Yes. Whoever put it there had to have known that Precious McFie was wearing that type of slipper when she walked the creek."

Susannah stood to go after the coffee carafe. She poured more coffee for them both, then returned the pot to the kitchen. "I'm listening," she called from the kitchen. "Go on."

"Okay," Kate said, reviewing the sequence of events even as she spoke. "We've got Precious McFie, heartbroken, walking in frigid weather in an attempt, it appears, to make herself very ill. We've got a prominent big-city family scandalized over what their children had done. We've got the former fiancé apparently coming to the side of his former beloved, who unbeknownst to him has fallen ill."

Susannah came back from the kitchen and sat down, giving Kate a half smile. "And he doesn't want to be seen, doesn't want his family to find out he's here," she said. "But if this is such a secretive visit, how did the reporter find out he came here?"

"Holden witnessed her death. I found an obscure mention that his name was on the death certificate."

Susannah grinned. "You're good," then she added, "But what does that have to do with what's going on now?"

Kate nodded. "That's where the story gets sketchy."

"How he was able to slip in and out of the hotel unnoticed, you mean?"

"Exactly."

"Why is this important?"

Kate pondered the question for a moment. "It occurs to me that some sort of secret passage might be the key to both mysteries—the hotel hauntings and the missing producer. Lots of dots to connect, only I haven't figured out how to connect them." Then she laughed lightly. "It's only a theory. Nothing else."

"Does your theory involve suspects you think might be involved in some sort of flimflam scam?"

"Flimflam scam?" Kate chuckled. "That's a good way to put it. And yes, I've got a suspect in mind. . . ."

Paul emerged from the bedroom. He'd showered and shaved and dressed for the day. Kate remembered that he had a breakfast meeting at the diner with the other pastors in town. She glanced at the clock, surprised at how the time had flown since Susannah's arrival.

Paul stopped to give Kate a kiss, greeted Susannah warmly, then headed to get some coffee. Sighs of ecstasy

emanated from the kitchen. He'd obviously spotted the cinnamon rolls.

With a roll in his hand, he came back through the doorway,
took a bite, then looked toward heaven as if the roll was manna
sent straight from God, and he was a starving Israelite.

After a few chews, he said, "Kate, I heard your cell beep
when I got out of the shower. It's in your handbag."

"Beep?"

"Yeah . . . I don't think I've ever heard it do that before."

Susannah returned to the kitchen with Paul while Kate
went to the bedroom to retrieve her phone. She picked it up,
frowning at the screen. It told her she had a new text message. She didn't know much about text messages and certainly didn't receive them very often.

She clicked on the READ NOW button, and the message
appeared. The Sender ID said "UNAVAILABLE," and under
the subject line was a single word: WARNING. Her gaze
traveled to the body of the message. It read:

STOP YOUR INVESTIGATION NOW. YOU DO
NOT WANT TO KNOW WHAT IS PLANNED FOR
YOU IF YOU DON'T. FORGET YOU HAVE EVER
HEARD OF PRECIOUS MCFIE. HER DEATH
WAS NOT ACCIDENTAL. AND NEITHER WILL
YOURS BE.

She stared at the words, trying to make sense of them,
then she slowly made her way to the kitchen. Her hand trembled as she passed the phone to Paul.

Chapter Nineteen

There were a half-dozen colors and at least as many designs spread out across Kate's worktable in her studio. It was Friday morning, and as soon as Paul left for Chattanooga to visit his mentor Nehemiah Jacobs, she had gone straight into the studio to work on a stained-glass votive for Susannah. Paul had expressed hesitance to leave after the ominous message Kate had received, but she assured him that she would be fine. She didn't want her incessant sleuthing to get in the way of Paul spending much-needed time with his mentor.

She chose a pattern of irises, which were Susannah's favorite flower, and monarch butterflies. The colors would be vivid, just like Susannah's personality. Kate went to work cutting the glass.

As she leaned over the table, she considered the Newt Keller case, the hotel hauntings, and the text-message threat from the previous day. Her heart skipped a beat every time she thought about it.

Paul had taken her phone to the deputy's office the previous morning, but because the place was still abuzz with the stepped-up search for Newt Keller, finding out the identity of the sender was obviously a low priority. Deputy Spencer also said the phone company couldn't block further messages from that ID because it was an unlisted number.

How did all these puzzle pieces fit together? It seemed that just when she thought she had figured out one part of the mystery, something else cropped up that completely changed the dynamics of the case.

Someone was worried that she was getting too close to the truth. But who?

She pressed the glass cutter and snipped a piece of violet glass, then she held it up to the light before trimming it to fit the space on the pattern. But her nagging thoughts kept her from concentrating as she should. She made two bad cuts, then laid the cutter down.

The threat obviously had to do with her investigation of Precious McFie's death. But why? Was there something she didn't know about the death? The text message said it wasn't accidental, but Kate suspected that was untrue, that the sender of the text message was simply trying to frighten her.

She picked up a piece of gold-hued glass and held it to the light, turning it slightly to determine the cut that would best complement the design.

She was back where she started, and the feeling she was missing something pecked away at her brain. But for the life of her, she couldn't figure out what it was.

She had just finished cutting the gold glass when the phone rang.

She trotted quickly into Paul's office, grabbed the receiver, and put it to her ear.

It was Renee.

"Our ghost has struck again," she said.

Kate sank into Paul's office chair. "Last night?"

"No, in broad daylight, this morning."

"At the hotel?"

"Yes. I was there for Birdie Birge's taping and saw it all."

Kate had spent the morning away from the studio to work on her gift for Susannah. She'd also just needed some time away to puzzle the mysteries. She sighed, thinking maybe she'd made the wrong choice. "What happened?"

Renee let out an annoyed sigh as if she thought Kate should've been there to see it firsthand.

"First the lights blinked and dimmed, then they blinked again and went out completely. Everything was shut down—in the studio, the kitchen . . . The entire hotel was without electricity."

"The power didn't go out here," Kate said. Her worktable light had been on all morning, without a flicker or a hiccup.

"Believe me, it did at the hotel," Renee said. "Then that same cold wind came up. That caught people's attention. And if that hadn't, the chair that moved across the foyer of its own accord would have."

"A chair moved itself across the foyer? That's impossible."

"I saw it with my own eyes."

Kate took a deep breath. "There's got to be a logical explanation."

Renee's voice took on its usual know-it-all tone. "Believe me, it was real. *Very* real. People were screaming and running outside. One woman fainted, and the fire department had to be called."

"What about the media? Were any reporters there to see it firsthand? Or camera crew to film it?"

"By this morning, most of the media had left. I guess they've moved on to the next story. There might have been one or two stray reporters hanging around, like Lucy Mae. I saw her interviewing some people, but she wasn't in the foyer when the chair moved." She paused, then said again, "I have no doubt that this is real."

Kate waited. Lately, she saw a different Renee than she was used to. Gone were the sarcastic remarks, the juicy gossip she was prone to spout, the police lingo, the well-placed, perfectly timed *harrumphs* that stood Kate's hair on end and made her pray for grace. Renee's brusque ways were somehow endearing, and truth be told, she missed them. It seemed the possibility of Copper Mill's ghost had frightened the spunk right out of her.

"What is it?" Kate prompted after an extended silence.

When Renee finally spoke, her voice trembled. "Something's wrong with Kisses. Really wrong with him."

"What do you mean?"

"I mean he's acting the same way he did when we saw the ghost at the hotel," Renee whispered as if worried that Kisses might hear her. "He yips and growls and runs in circles all over the house like some ghost is playing with him—you know, with some sort of ghostly Frisbee that people can't see. I'm certain that a ghost from the hotel—or maybe a different one—has moved in here."

Kate could hear sniffling on the other end of the line.

"It may be something else entirely," Kate said. "Why don't you try the vet?"

A harrumph erupted on the other end of the line. "You wouldn't say that if you could see him right now. Listen to this."

Kate waited, then heard yipping and growling and Caroline praying.

Renee came back on the line. "See what I mean?"

"It certainly doesn't sound like the Kisses we all know and love."

Renee said she would think about calling the vet, then they said their good-byes, and Kate pressed the off button.

The ghost of the Hamilton Springs Hotel was definitely becoming more active. Whipping up a frigid wind. Pushing a guest down the stairs. Leaving ballet-slipper prints upstairs. Cutting off the electricity. Moving furniture around.

Things seemed to be escalating, and it was time for Kate to act.

Kate grabbed her coat and handbag and headed to the garage. She went straight to Paul's tackle box, rummaged around, and grabbed a spool of fishing line.

Chapter Twenty

Kate raced into the hotel. The power was still out, which meant the tapings were canceled, and the foyer was eerily empty. She headed straight to Sybil's office.

The general manager gave Kate a weary smile. As she walked into the dark office, she motioned for Kate to sit down across from her desk.

"I heard what happened here this morning," Kate said.

Sybil nodded. "It was quite a show. And I've decided the ghost of the Hamilton Springs Hotel has won at last."

"What do you mean?"

"I've just finished writing my resignation letter." She gestured toward an old-fashioned typewriter behind her. "I'm calling corporate to let them know that today's my last day."

"Oh dear," Kate said, stricken. "I think I'm onto something that will explain everything. Can you give it just a few more days?"

Everything might be a stretch, but Kate could hope—and maybe pass along a bit of that hope to Sybil.

"It's been an agonizing decision. In many ways, this hotel is my life. But the stress is too great—and honestly, Kate, at first I thought it was a hoax. But after the theatrics this morning, I'm convinced the haunting is real."

"I'm so sorry," Kate said quietly.

"I've talked with my boss at corporate, letting him know why I must leave. He's quite upset over it all, especially the lost revenue the hauntings have caused. But he'll be sending a replacement. We're hoping that person can turn things around." She shrugged. "I'm beginning to think our ghost has something personal against me."

"Occupancy is down . . . Is that the reason for the drop in revenue?"

Sybil nodded. "Aside from the Taste Network guests, the hotel is practically empty. Other than the network people, guests have even stopped coming to the Bristol. And the spa has lost customers and once the Taste people are gone, they plan to lay off their masseuse. At this rate, we'll go under in a few months." She let out a hollow laugh. "The ironic thing is I'd hoped that letting the Taste Network film here would give us a needed boost. I thought it was a brilliant marketing move. How could I have been so wrong? My brilliant idea obviously angered the ghost that haunts this place. The whole thing backfired. The Taste Network ratings have gone through the roof, while the Hamilton Springs may have to close its doors."

"What if the two things are connected—the ratings spike and the ghost activity?"

"That's what I just said; they are connected."

"No, that's not what I meant. What if the ghost activity was generated by someone in the network, someone who had a lot to gain from the media attention?"

Sybil sighed and shook her head. "I've thought about that as well. It doesn't make sense. Rumors of the ghost have been around for decades. But this is real. If this was a one-time occurrence, I'd agree that someone is pulling off some sort of a hoax. But, rumor or reality, it's about to put us under."

"Can you show me the chair that moved across the foyer this morning?"

"I don't know what for, but, of course, you can take a look. I examined it after the event and didn't see anything unusual. It's just a sturdy, handmade wooden chair with a cushion." She stood to lead the way to the foyer.

A few minutes later, Kate knelt beside the chair, felt around the legs and back, looked underneath the cushion, tipped it this way and that, then pulled out her penlight and peered underneath the chair.

"This chair would be too heavy to move easily," she said. "It would take something incredibly strong to even move it a few inches. And you said it moved several feet?"

"From the center of the foyer to the staircase on the right."

"Did it remain on the floor, or did it levitate a bit?"

"It remained on the floor. Why?"

Kate looked up at Sybil. "Because I would come closer to believing that a ghost moved it if it floated across the room. But this floor is polished wood, a very nice slick surface for sliding furniture, I would think."

Sybil's expression changed. "True," she said and knelt beside Kate. "But it would have to have been pulled by something invisible."

Kate played the beam of the penlight up and down all four legs of the chair. "I see some deep cuts on two legs, as if someone notched the wood to keep a tie or pulley of some sort from sliding off. They're fresh cuts, not something that might have happened when the chair was made."

"I see them," Sybil breathed. "But what could be strong enough, and yet invisible, to move something this heavy."

"I'm guessing a filament of some sort. Something similar to fishing line."

A slow smile dawned on Sybil's face. "You're good."

Kate grinned. "Thanks, but we haven't proven anything yet." She reached into her purse and pulled out a roll of fishing line. "Let's try it out."

A few minutes later, Kate knelt behind the reception desk and slowly reeled in the filament they had just tied to the chair.

"But I can see the fishing line," Sybil called to her as the chair moved across the floor.

"That's because you were looking for it." Kate stood and untied the line. "What else was going on when the chair moved?"

"The lights had just flickered and gone out."

"Aha! A sleight of hand. Everyone was distracted by the power failure, saw the chair moving on its own, and jumped to conclusions."

"What about the cold wind? How could that be faked?"

"Did you feel the wind?"

She nodded. "And I saw the drapes move, yet no one was near them."

Kate walked over to the nearest large window and lifted the drape. "There's nothing here now, but it would be easy to place fans behind each one and set them on a timer to go off at exactly the same time."

Sybil's smile was even wider. "And the wind? Did we imagine it because of the fans?"

"Partially," Kate said. "But someone could have turned on the AC at precisely the right moment. Added a chill to an already cold fall day. Dry ice and fans might also cause the same phenomenon."

"The AC theory is possible, I suppose, but I'm the only one with a key to the heating-and-cooling systems."

"Maintenance doesn't have access?"

"They come to me for the key."

"How long has it been since you've seen your key?"

"It's in my desk. I see it every d—" Then she blinked. "Come to think of it . . ." Without finishing, she turned and hurried back down the hall to her office.

Kate followed along after her, reaching the office at the same time Sybil pulled open her desk drawer.

She rummaged around in the drawer for a moment, then looked up at Kate. "The key is gone," she said.

Without another word, she reached for the resignation letter on her desk, tore it in half, and dropped it in the wastebasket.

"It's time to declare war," she said, grinning. "It's about time I took charge of my own hotel again."

Kate chuckled. "Count me among your soldiers."

"I believe you're the general in this war," Sybil said with a mock salute. Both women laughed.

KATE SWUNG BY RENEE'S on her way home from the hotel.

"How is Kisses?" Kate asked when a haggard-looking Caroline opened the door.

"More importantly, how am I?" Caroline said. "And I'm exhausted, thank you. We struggled for a half hour to get him into his tote. That ghost had him barking and growling to beat the band. Finally had to ask one of the Jenner boys down the street to come over and help." She shook her head. "Renee took Little Umpkins"—she rolled her eyes at the nickname— "to the vet's, though I don't know what good it will do."

"I'm sorry it's been such a trial, Caroline. Will you tell Renee I stopped by? I'll check in later to see what the vet said."

"I don't hold much hope that the vet can do anything. I've already called Father Lucas at St. Lucy's to set up a prayer meeting. Left the message on his answering machine, but he hasn't returned the call."

Kate stifled a smile as she imagined Lucas Gregory's reaction. She wondered if he'd ever had such a request before. "Well, let me know what he says."

"You can come if you'd like."

"To the prayer meeting?" She coughed to cover her mouth, and the giggle that threatened to spill out. "Okay, well, let me know . . ." she finally managed.

Five minutes later, Kate turned down her street. Then, puzzled, she slowed the Honda as she neared the parsonage.

The sheriff's black-and-white SUV was parked across the street, and two other unmarked cars were parked on either side of Susannah's star coach. She suspected the unmarked cars belonged to FBI agents.

She pulled behind the SUV and parked. Heart racing, she went up to the coach. She had just started up the stairs when the door whooshed opened and Sheriff Roberts stepped out. Behind him was a teary-eyed Susannah, in handcuffs. Following on her heels was her attorney and two FBI agents. Last to come down the steps was Skip Spencer, looking very grave.

"Susannah!" Kate tried to move closer to her friend, but the agents blocked her way.

"What's going on?" she demanded of anyone who would answer. No one did.

They led Susannah to the sheriff's vehicle and, opening the back door, deposited her inside.

"Oh, Sheriff Roberts, this is a terrible mistake," Kate said. "Please, don't arrest her."

The sheriff gestured for Kate to follow him to one side.

"I know she's your friend and you want to protect her. But a witness has come forward who saw her with Newt Keller at the place where his vehicle was discovered."

Kate felt as if she'd been socked in the stomach. "A witness?" she whispered. Then she frowned. "That's still circumstantial."

His expression was kind when he said, "There's more. And it isn't circumstantial."

Kate's heart threatened to stop beating. "More?" The word came out in a whisper.

"We received the reports back from the blood sample on the seat. It matches blood found on a hand towel in the trunk of her sports car."

Kate's hand flew to her mouth. "Oh no!"

"I've probably said too much, but as I said before, I know you're her friend."

Kate went over to the SUV and looked at her friend, who was sitting in the back.

"Is it true, Susannah?"

Susannah nodded, and as tears slid down her cheeks, she turned her gaze away from Kate's.

Chapter Twenty-One

There had been another time, long ago, when Susannah had been driven away in a car. She had cried that day too. The girls were high-school juniors, with the promise of the best year of their friendship ahead.

Susannah had just auditioned—and landed—the lead role in *Our Town*, to be put on by their high school for the whole San Antonio community. Kate had also tried out but didn't make the cut. She ended up as production manager, a role she realized she was better suited for even though she'd initially been disappointed that she hadn't landed a part in the play.

Her friend had come a long way from the shy little girl who had moved into the house across the street from Kate.

Susannah was an only child whose parents believed that children should be seen, not heard. They thought of themselves as intellectual. Her father was a biology professor at a small private college, and her mother was a homemaker whose greatest pastime was reading the classics. They both wanted Susannah to fit into their mold of likes and dislikes.

Television wasn't allowed in her family. Neither was any music, except classical.

But Susannah wasn't anything like her parents. The first day she visited the Blume family, she gaped in wide-eyed wonder.

Games and projects were scattered in every nook and cranny, from jigsaw puzzles to Tinkertoy towns to games like Candy Land and Chutes and Ladders. Against one wall stood an old upright piano with an uncovered keyboard that welcomed anyone to sit down and play.

Margaret Blume, Kate's mother, taught piano lessons, sang in the church choir, and led the local Brownie troop. She was completely devoted to letting Kate fall in love with all the good things life had to offer. Even as Kate thought back on those years, she pictured her mom as a gently clucking hen who gathered Kate, and any others that came along, holding them close and teaching them about unconditional love through actions, not words.

Scott Blume, Kate's father, was a big man, quieter than her mother but just as expressive in his love for his family and for God.

Kate's mother loved to cook, and there was always enough food to feed anyone Kate might bring to the dinner table.

Kate still remembered the day her mother noticed a shy little Susannah watching her with big eyes as she fixed the sauce for a pot of spaghetti. She pulled up a chair for Kate to watch, then grabbed a kitchen chair, stood Susannah on the top, and put a wooden spoon in her hand. "You'll just need to stir so it doesn't stick," she said.

"That's too hard." The seven-year-old frowned with worry. "I don't know if I can."

"Cooking is easy if you just follow directions. Just one step at a time, just one ingredient at a time. When the meat is a nice golden brown, we'll add some salt and pepper." She then let a grinning Susannah sprinkle the shakers over the mixture.

Kate's mother took a little spoonful out and placed it in a small dish with a spoon. "Now taste this and see if it needs anything." It was obvious Susannah had never been assigned such a task before. She blinked, looking uncertain. Margaret laughed. "Like more salt maybe?"

Susannah scrunched her face as she put a spoonful of the crumbled hamburger into her mouth. Then she closed her eyes, taking Margaret's directions very seriously. "*Mmm*," she finally said. "It's good."

"No more salt then?"

"No." Susannah blinked as if she couldn't believe someone actually accepted her opinion.

"How about pepper?"

Susannah tasted again. "Yes," she said, obviously getting into the spirit of what needed to be done. "It needs more pepper."

"All right, now," Kate's mother said seriously. "Next you'll need to make the sauce."

"Me? By myself?"

"Of course. I'll open the cans of tomato sauce, and you can pour them into the pan when you think the hamburger is golden brown."

Susannah did as instructed, every once in a while sneaking a peek at Kate to see if she was watching. Next, Margaret put some little red and white tins on the counter by the stove.

"Have you ever heard of oregano?"

Susannah shook her head.

"Smell this. It's something you'll use a lot when you're cooking, especially Italian food." She placed measuring spoons on the counter within reach of the child standing on the chair in front of the stove.

"This is Italian food?" Susannah's eyes widened. "Real Italian food?" She took a whiff of the oregano and laughed. "It smells good."

"Yes, it is, though real Italians could probably show us an even better way to make it."

"I don't think it could ever be better than this," Susannah said, her eyes shining.

"And now some thyme," Margaret said, handing the tin to Susannah to sniff. "And rosemary . . . and sweet basil . . . and a bay leaf, crumbled just so."

Susannah's reaction was the same with each new ingredient. Her hand shook with excitement as she carefully measured a spoonful of each ingredient and sprinkled it into the meat mixture. It was as if Margaret was opening a brand-new world to the child, a world Susannah had no idea existed until she stepped inside the Blume house.

As Kate thought back on that day, watching her mother gather the lonely little girl from the sterile house across the street into her arms, she remembered the fragrance of the kitchen as Susannah put all the ingredients together to make her first pasta sauce. She remembered hearing somewhere that smells can bring back memories faster than any other sense.

But as she remembered the wonderful aroma of spices and herbs, of tomatoes and onions and garlic, it seemed to her that it was also the fragrance of love.

Susannah practically lived at their house from that day on. She confided in Margaret through the awkward growing-up years, even though Kate's mother tried to help Susannah and her mother build better communication skills.

Then, abruptly, ten years later, on a rainy autumn day, Susannah ran across the street to the Blumes'. She fell into Margaret's arms, crying.

"We have to move," she said. "To Atlanta."

Kate started to cry with her. "You can't go!"

Susannah pulled back, sniffling. "My dad just got a new teaching job at a university in Atlanta. He and Mom say they've been waiting for a long time for an opportunity like this. They say it will change our lives." She shook her head and reached for the hankie Margaret handed her. "But they never told *me*." She looked first at Kate's mother, then at Kate. "Why didn't they tell me this could happen? All my plans, the lead role in the play . . . and it means nothing to them. It's like . . . I don't matter."

"Maybe you can stay with us," Kate suggested.

Her mother nodded. "If your parents would allow it, you'd be welcome to live with us so you can finish out the year—or at least finish the semester so you can be in the play."

But Susannah's parents said no. They thanked the Blumes for offering, but her mother explained that she and Susannah's father felt the move would be a growing experi-ence for their daughter. "Hardships can do much to toughen the spirit," she had said.

Looking back on it, Kate wondered if there had also been some jealousy involved. Maybe Susannah's mother simply wanted her daughter back.

Just three weeks later, the moving van parked in front of the house, and when the furniture was loaded, Susannah crossed the street one last time. She hugged everyone in the Blume family, saving Kate till last.

"Best friends forever," she whispered.

Kate tried hard to be brave for Susannah's sake. She blinked back the sting in her eyes and, clutching Susannah's hand, whispered, "Best friends forever and ever."

Susannah's dad backed out of the garage and beeped his horn.

Susannah crawled into the backseat, and looking at Kate, a tear slid down her cheek, just as it had as she sat in back of the sheriff's SUV.

Chapter Twenty-Two

A half hour after Susannah was taken away, the doorbell rang, and Kate hurried from her studio to answer it.

Joe Tucker stood on the porch, his shoulders slumped, his expression full of sorrow. He held an old hat in his hands and played with the brim as he spoke.

"Is Paul here?"

"He's in Chattanooga, Joe. Is there anything I can do for you?"

He shook his head. "I know Miz Applebaum is your friend, and I held off saying anything to the sheriff as long as I could. But I saw what I saw, and I had to get it off my chest."

"Oh, Joe, you're the witness they told me about?"

He nodded. "I was on my way home from the taping that day when I saw this silver sports car headin' up Smith Street toward the creek. It's unusual to see a tiny vehicle like that on a rough road, and I'd remembered seein' the same car the night before, when the Taste Network folks got here. Saw Miz Applebaum get out of it, so I knew it was hers. Anyway, when I saw the car, I followed it just in case it bottomed out or something, and she needed help. That's when I saw

Miz Applebaum get out and lay into the owner of the Hummer. They were arguin' to beat the band. I figured it was none of my business, so I hightailed it out of there as fast as I could."

Kate let the information soak in, feeling her spirits spiral downward. Why hadn't Susannah told her she was with Newt Keller that day? There could only be one reason: she had something to hide.

"You did what you had to do, Joe. Please don't think I'll hold it against you. It was the right thing to do."

He looked relieved. "I hope it all turns out okay."

She touched his arm. "It will."

She waited until he was gone before she cried.

A STORM MOVED INTO Copper Mill that afternoon. The wind whistled through the trees, and blasts of frigid air rattled branches against the windows. It reminded Kate of the storm that took the life of Precious McFie. She attempted to get back to the stained-glass votive she was making for Susannah, but her thoughts were anywhere but on her work.

Finally, she gave up and called Livvy to see if she would like to join her for coffee and pie at the diner.

"I was just getting ready to call you, Kate. We've seen too little of each other lately," Livvy said. "It'll be good to catch up."

By the time Kate backed out of the garage, the rain had started, large drops at first, then it came faster and harder, strong winds driving it at a slant against the windshield.

When she got out of the car at the diner, the street was already slick with sleet.

"And it's not even winter yet," LuAnne said when Kate stepped inside.

Livvy waved from a booth by the window, and Kate made her way toward her across the nearly full diner. Several tables were filled with Taste Network cast and crew, who apparently had the day off because of the power outage at the hotel. A few recognized Kate and called out their greetings.

In the back of the diner, Birdie Birge was holding court with Daryl Gallagher and Armand Platt, who, judging from his animated conversation, seemed delighted to have the afternoon off from his chef's duties. Kate wondered if he would be out of a job soon. How quickly circumstances had changed since he jokingly offered Susannah a job at the Bristol.

If things didn't turn around quickly at the Hamilton Springs, Armand wouldn't be the only one out of a job.

Livvy touched Kate's hand. "I heard about the arrest."

"News travels fast," Kate remarked.

"It always does in Copper Mill," Livvy said gently. "I'm so sorry. Are you okay?"

She nodded. "I just wish there was something I could do."

"Have you talked to Susannah?" Livvy asked. "This must be terribly hard on her."

"I called Skip Spencer to see if I could get in to see her, but they're still questioning her. I asked about bail, and he didn't know." Kate leaned across the table toward Livvy. "Her career may already be damaged beyond repair."

Just then a cell phone rang across the diner. Nicolette stood, and even from the distance between them, Kate could see the flush on her cheeks as she lifted the phone to her ear. She said something to the group she was with, then, still holding the phone, she strode out of the diner.

Kate pulled back the curtain and watched Nicolette walk

across the street. Then, stopping, she leaned against a lamp-post and smiled as she continued talking.

Watching the scene along with Kate, Livvy said, "It appears to be good news."

"More than that," Kate said, leaning forward. "Look at her face. What expression do you see?"

Livvy frowned, then a slow realization seemed to dawn. Her eyes were wide when she looked back at Kate.

"That's the face of a woman in love," Kate said. "And I'm pretty sure I know who she's in love with . . ."—she refrained from giving the air a victory punch—"and who she's talking to."

Livvy laughed. "Something tells me you just connected some dots."

"One big dot," Kate said.

They finished their pie, then Livvy said, "Don't forget. Tomorrow night is the book signing."

"I wouldn't miss it."

"Is Paul coming?"

"He's decided we need to support the library—and you—in this. We'll both be there early, just in case you need us."

Livvy pressed her fork into the last of her pie crust, took a bite, and smiled. "To help with crowd control?"

"Are the Caspers still planning to picket?"

"I think so. I was hoping that the fuss would die down . . . until the strange events at the hotel hit. Now I fear it just riled up the Caspers and Ghostbusters even more."

LuAnne brought their bill, and the two women went over to the cash register to pay. "Even if it's just for moral support, we'll be there."

"Thank you."

"And, of course, there's Joel St. Nicklaus, who's probably dealt with this sort of thing before. He'll know how to handle the naysayers."

"Maybe he's got something magical in his bag of tricks."

Kate groaned. "Oh dear. Next we'll be talking about his white beard."

Livvy stared at her friend for a moment, then bit her bottom lip.

"Don't tell me . . ."

Livvy giggled. "I've seen his photo, and, yes, he's got one. But he looks more like Hemingway than the other white-bearded guy."

Outside the diner, Livvy patted Kate's hand. "Try not to worry about Susannah. God's got her in his hands, and he's not going to let go."

"I know that in here," Kate said, tapping her heart, "but it's up here that's prone to worry." She touched her forehead. "Especially when it's someone I care about." She didn't mention the text message she'd received, though that worried her as well.

They hugged good-bye, and Livvy headed back to the library. Kate rounded the corner to where she had parked the Honda.

She came to a dead stop.

Nicolette was standing in front of her car, arms crossed.

"I saw you watching me," she said, tilting her head toward the diner widow. "It wasn't a casual glance. You pulled back the curtain and stared while I was on the phone."

Kate's heart did a little dance, and she coughed to get the

rhythm back to normal. "I noticed the glow on your face and wondered who you might be talking to," she said.

"Glow?" The word came out as a growl.

"Yes. The glow of a woman who cares a great deal about the person she's talking to."

Nicolette looked stunned. Then she laughed. "You have a very active imagination."

Kate didn't answer. Her heart was still pounding. She swallowed hard and tried to breathe normally.

"No matter." Nicolette shrugged. "But I would like to pass along a word of warning. You're very nosy. I suggest you mind your own business."

"So you decided to deliver the warning in person this time?"

Nicolette looked momentarily confused. "I don't know what you're talking about." The smirk returned. "Now, if you'll excuse me."

Even though the sleet had stopped falling, a cold wind still blasted, lifting Kate's hair, stinging her cheeks, and chilling her to the bone.

KATE TOOK A CHANCE that she might be able to talk with Susannah and stopped by the jail. Skip Spencer led her into the holding facility.

Susannah sat on the side of a bunk, alone in her cell. It broke Kate's heart to see her this way.

She looked up when she heard Kate's approach. Her smile was wan.

"Hey, kiddo. How are you doing?"

"Fair to middlin'," she said with a hollow laugh.

Skip returned to his desk, leaving Kate to speak with her friend.

"Is it true?" Kate asked again, hoping for a different answer. "About the blood on the towel, I mean?"

"Yes. I went on a drive that day, spotted Newt's Hummer, and decided to give him a piece of my mind about how he treats people. I drove to that place by the creek, got out of my car and found him sitting in his. He seemed despondent, which surprised me. I saw him holding that Swiss army knife of his and panicked."

She shook her head as she walked toward the bars between them. "I thought he was going to harm himself. So I lunged—tried to take it away from him." She sighed. "My vivid imagination got the best of me. But I missed and during the scuffle, he cut himself. I ran for a towel, dabbed it on his wound." She shrugged. "We even had a laugh over it, and then I left. Without giving it another thought, I tossed the towel in the trunk."

"I wish you'd told me that from the beginning," Kate said quietly.

"I didn't think it was a big deal," Susannah said, blinking back her tears. "But apparently it is."

"It is to the police," Kate whispered, touching Susannah's hand through the bars.

"That's what worries me." Susannah turned her back and Kate could see that she was crying.

Chapter Twenty-Three

Kate and Paul drove to the library a half hour before the book signing was due to start. A few Caspers had already arrived with their picket signs. They were in full uniform, florals, plaids and pastel sateens.

An older man held a Ghostbuster's sign, and beside him stood the waitress named Sophie from the diner. She held a Casper sign.

On Sophie's other side was a tiny woman in a wheelchair. Though her hair was white, the shape of her face was identical to Sophie's. She held a sign that said, "I believe!" in the center of an outline of Casper, the Friendly Ghost. Tied to the back of her wheelchair was a bunch of white balloons, which she handed, one at a time, to people as they arrived for the signing.

"That's Sophie and her grandparents," Kate said. "They have a live-in ghost that moves furniture, puts away dishes, and covers people with blankets so they won't get cold."

Paul laughed. "That's the kind of ghost I'd like to have."

"I have a feeling I know their ghost personally."

"Sophie?"

"You guessed it, though she didn't say it in so many words. And I understand Sophie's reasons for 'ghosting.'"

Still sitting in the Honda, they fell silent for a moment, watching as a few other Caspers marched to the front of the library, interspersed with people holding Ghostbuster signs.

"Do you think it helped when you spoke with the folks at Faith Briar about ghosts and the possibility of their existence?"

"People seemed to just need to talk about it. Some were genuinely concerned but others were caught up in the frenzy caused by the St. Nicklaus book. And, of course, the idea that the Hamilton Springs has its own ghost seemed to push some of our parishioners over the edge." He paused. "But it's not over yet. We've got some mighty upset folks around town. I wouldn't be surprised to see a better turnout than we expected tonight."

"I just hope there aren't any rowdy ghosties that interrupt the author . . . or the storyteller."

"Ghosties?" Paul quirked a brow.

"We have foodies, Tasties, roadies . . . Why not ghosties?" Kate turned to Paul. "You're still planning to speak to them?"

His expression was solemn as he nodded. "The whole town is questioning the existence of ghosts. I can't just let it go without saying a word."

"And we did promise Livvy we'd try to help."

They got out of the car, and Paul headed to the front of the library and held up his hands. Immediately, the hubbub quieted and everyone turned toward him.

"Friends, I know you've all got questions about all this, and honestly I do too. Some of you believe with all your heart that there's such a thing as ghosts. Others of you believe just as strongly there isn't.

"But I want to remind you that focusing on the ghosts, whether you believe in them or not, takes our focus off the more important things—how we treat one another, for one thing. How we see God's work in *our* lives—not whether ghostly apparitions exist or not. We know our God is real, and I think we may need reminding that it's Him we need to keep our sights on. His work in our lives as we reflect his love to others."

Paul's gesture was all inclusive. "All of us here have the opportunity to accept each other even in our differences, even as God accepts us unconditionally. Of course, we can't always agree on everything, but we can agree to disagree." He grinned. "I know that's been said before, but it's worth repeating."

In the back of the crowd, the grandmother in the wheel-chair shouted, "Hear hear!"

A smattering of others applauded, then the clapping grew louder. A Casper hugged a Ghostbuster. Then several more did the same. Soon there were more hugs, chatting and laughter.

Paul looked at Kate and grinned again. She gave him a thumbs up.

A late-model Ford pulled up just then and a man of about fifty got out of the driver's side, then went around to the passenger side and opened the door.

"I believe that's Joel St. Nicklaus," Paul said.

"He fits the description," Kate agreed. "And that must be our storyteller with him."

"How about we greet them and escort them in?" Paul said.

He took Kate's hand as they moved toward the author and his companion.

There wasn't an empty seat in the reading area when seven o'clock rolled around. Livvy introduced the speakers— Joel St. Nicklaus and the storyteller, Maggie McFie Waterhouse —then sat down between her husband Danny and Kate, who were seated in the front row.

Joel spoke first, entertaining the audience with stories about why he chose the topic for his book and the rich materials he found during his research—the stories about haunted houses, hotels, and shops—and how he embellished them for the book.

"There are more ghost stories out there than one can imagine," he said, then looked startled when the Caspers cheered and jabbed their "I Believe!" signs in the air.

He spoke for fifteen minutes, reminded people that they could buy his book at the back table after the storyteller was through speaking, then turned the program over to Maggie.

Kate was taken with the woman immediately. She appeared to be in her forties, very petite, with dark cascading curls drawn away from her face. She wore a white gauzy dress with a midcalf handkerchief hem. Kate noticed that balletlike slippers graced her feet, and when she moved, it seemed she was almost dancing.

Maggie gave a slight tilt of the head to someone standing at the back of the room, and the lights dimmed. Kate blinked. In the twilightlike light, the woman took on an almost ethereal visage.

"My name is Precious McFie." Maggie's voice was that of

a young woman, breathless and beckoning. The kind of voice that immediately drew Kate back in time.

She delved into the story, and in telling it in first person, she became Precious McFie. There wasn't a sound in the room except her voice as she spoke of the love of her life, her upcoming marriage, the joy that filled her heart when she thought of her beloved, Holden Giles III.

"Then one day," she said, her voice taking on a haunting quality, filled with sorrow and desperate sadness, "my beloved was no more. I say no more because he might as well have been dead to me. He found another love and discarded me like rubbish."

Maggie told of the journey by train to Copper Mill, a place her family and his had often come on holiday. The elegant Copper Creek Hotel was to have been her vacation destination, she said, and after her love left, the place drew her as sure as a moth was drawn to a candle flame.

"I brought with me my wedding gown and slippers," Maggie said, twirling. Her gossamer skirt suddenly became the gown, and her ballet slippers, the wedding shoes. She lifted a silk scarf to her head, and as she again twirled, it became her veil.

"I waited for my love, thinking surely he would change his mind and come to me. But he didn't, at least not right away. And when he did, it was too late."

She went on with the details of Holden's journey to Copper Mill—how, in the end, it was Precious he wanted.

She told of her walk by the creek in the sleet and hail, wearing only her wedding gown; at the same time, unknown to her, Holden was on a train destined for Copper Mill.

She became ill that night, but as she hovered near death, she looked up and saw Holden's face. "At first I thought it was an apparition," Maggie said. "I didn't believe that he had actually come to me. He pledged me his love, he pledged to never leave me, and he begged me not to die.

"His visits were a secret, you see. Nobody knew he was with me, not even the hotel staff. His father had political ambitions, and Holden told me that his scandalous behavior would harm the family, and most especially, his father's bid for governor.

"It came to me that night that my Holden was not the man I thought he was. I was nearly delirious with fever, but not so ill that I couldn't see the real reason Holden wanted his presence kept a secret. He was still in love with the other woman. Whatever his ties to me, they were borne more of guilt than of love.

"I tried to send him away, but he would not leave me. He sat by my bed, watching me as I struggled for breath, watching me as I slipped into unconsciousness, watching me die.

"You might wonder how I knew about his comings and goings, how he managed to creep into my room undetected by the hotel staff and even the doctor.

"I seemed to float above the bed before I drew my last breath. I remember floating through walls and closed doors as if they were not there. Holden, in his obsessive desire to keep his presence unknown, used a secret vehicle for his own purposes. . . ."

Kate gasped.

Maggie McFie Waterhouse had just connected a major dot in the puzzle. Kate glanced at Paul to see if he'd noticed, but he was as mesmerized as the rest of the audience. Then she looked at Livvy. Her friend was also staring straight ahead, apparently unaware of the clue Maggie had unknowingly dropped into Kate's lap.

She barely heard the rest of Maggie's story, as her mind connected the dots: Newt's Swiss Army knife in the Hummer, a knife he never let anyone else use; Nicolette's phone call from someone who made her face glow; a "vehicle" for getting from one floor to another; lights flickering on and off in the ghost wing of the hotel.

Haunted? Hardly. Kate had a pretty good idea why it wasn't.

Chapter Twenty-Four

T onight's the night all of this will end," Kate said to Livvy.
She had stopped by the library to return some books
on ghosts and hauntings, pro and con, that Paul had borrowed.
As soon as Livvy saw her, she said it was break time and suggested they grab a cup of tea at the diner.

They sat at a booth by the window—the same window
where Kate had seen Nicolette on the phone and put two and
two together about who was on the other end.

"I'm almost positive that Newt Keller is hiding out, and I
think I know where. It's time to confront him." She lowered
her voice. "I don't care if it takes all night; I'm going to wait
for him and see that justice is done."

"Where?"

She smiled. "He's been under our noses the whole time.
I'm convinced he's at the Hamilton Springs."

Livvy grew even more alarmed. "Oh, Kate!"

Kate nodded. "I can't wait any longer, Liv. I have to find
out the truth."

"Then at least call the sheriff and let him know what
you're up to."

"I tried to get through to him this afternoon. I told Skip what I'd discovered. He said he'd pass along the information."

LuAnne stopped by their table. "Sorry for the wait, girls. We're slammed today, what with the hotel out of commission and all. What can I do you for?"

"A slice of lemon-meringue pie for me," Livvy said. "And tea."

"Make that two," Kate said.

LuAnne came back with a teapot, then bent conspiratorially toward them and dropped her voice. "Did you hear what happened at the hotel this morning?"

"Something new?" Kate couldn't imagine what else was going on at the Hamilton Springs. The previous week's supposed haunting was still the talk of the town.

"Well, I overheard some talk just now—and I won't mention which table I was listening to—but the word is that the former Ms. Keller is hoppin' mad because for five years she's been trying to win Mr. Keller back. Apparently, she thought she'd almost convinced him to give their relationship another try when he disappeared, and now she's blaming Susannah for losin' him again."

"They're divorced," Kate said, incredulous. It made sense now that Jacqueline Keller flew in from Europe to search for him. She had the financial well-being of the company on her shoulders. What didn't make sense was why she would want such an ogre back. Then again, one woman's ogre was often another woman's prince. Apparently, Nicolette Pascal also thought him a prince.

"And that's not all," LuAnne continued. "She's ordered

everyone in the network to move out of the hotel until this 'issue is settled'—her words, according to my sources. And apparently, they were glad to go."

"Where will they go?"

LuAnne waggled her fingers. "Motels and hotels outside town. Apparently, they've decided to shoot those off-location shots in the meantime."

Kate sipped her tea as a howling blast of wind rattled some tree branches outside.

The door to the diner burst opened with a bang, and Renee Lambert, umbrella unfurled, arrived like Mary Poppins on another gust of wind. She slipped off her coat, spotted Livvy and Kate, and headed toward them, wrapping her umbrella on the way. The long strap of Kisses' tote was slung over one shoulder.

"I saw your car outside, Kate, and thought I'd stop by with my news."

"About Kisses?"

"Turns out there isn't a ghost living with us after all."

Kate avoided exchanging glances with Livvy. "What did the vet say was the problem?"

"I added some new health foods to his diet recently, and apparently, well, to put it delicately, the new food caused him to be, well, you know . . ."

"Ah yes," Kate said, stifling a grin. "I can imagine."

"Flatulent?" Livvy filled in, ever the wordsmith.

Kate couldn't resist any longer. She shot Livvy a smile, and the twitch at the corner of her friend's mouth—just before she covered it with her napkin—said that giggles were threatening to erupt.

"Yes," Renee sighed. "My poor Little Umpkins."

Kate's cell chirped from deep in her handbag. LuAnne returned to the kitchen to put in their order, and Kate dug for the phone.

She found it, flipped it open, then bit her lip. "Oh no," she breathed, her heart sinking.

"What is it?" Livvy asked.

Kate read the text message, then handed the phone to Livvy. Renee sidled closer, glanced around the room, lowered her voice, then read it aloud over Livvy's shoulder. "Be certain you are being watched," she whispered. "Stop your investigation now or you will be sorry."

"Well, if that doesn't take the cake," Renee said, turning pale. She dropped into the booth across from Kate.

"Oh, Kate," Livvy said, handing back the phone.

"One thing I know. Threats aren't going to stop me from trying to find Newt. It's the only way we can get to the bottom of this."

Livvy sat back. "I'm worried about all of this, Kate. You shouldn't be alone at that deserted hotel trying to find him."

Kate thought about Livvy's words. It was one thing to put herself in harm's way, but in light of the most recent text message, she couldn't ask Livvy to do the same. Besides, what if her theory was wrong?

"I've got it covered, Livvy."

Renee had remained uncharacteristically silent through Kate's interchange with Livvy. When LuAnne appeared a few minutes later with two plates of lemon-meringue pie, Renee stood abruptly, collected the tote with snoring Kisses, and said she had some errands to run. She left without saying good-bye and nearly forgot to grab her coat and umbrella.

Chapter Twenty-Five

It was nearing eleven o'clock when Kate headed the Honda into the Hamilton Springs parking lot. Paul had fallen asleep, and she'd left a note, telling him where she'd gone.

The lot was empty, and the hotel was nearly dark, even though the power had started working again a few hours earlier. The restaurant, tearoom, spa, and hotel had apparently remained closed after the most recent ghost activities.

The wind moaned as Kate exited the car, and an icy sting of rain blasted into her face. She caught her breath and tied the belt on her coat tighter, dropping the hood over her head.

She trotted to the entrance, trying not to think about how vulnerable she was in a deserted hotel at night. Except for the howling wind, it was eerily quiet, a stark contrast to the hubbub when the network people were there.

Her hands shook as she reached for the door. A single light glowed from somewhere behind the front desk, where the reservation people would normally be seated, smiling cheerfully at guests as they entered the hotel.

But that night, there was no one.

Kate opened the door and made her way across the foyer. She prayed that Sybil would be in her office. They had talked on the phone earlier, and Sybil had assured her that she would be waiting. The thought helped calm her jittery nerves.

But what if Sybil wasn't there? Kate didn't want to consider that she might be alone in the abandoned building. She pushed the thought from her mind and knocked on Sybil's office door and waited for an answer.

There was none.

Her legs were starting to shake. Ignoring them as best she could, she reached for the knob, turned it, and eased the door inward an inch or so, just enough to see that Sybil wasn't at her desk.

Kate backed slowly out of the room as cold fingers of fear began to travel up her spine. She let out a deep breath, then sucked in another before she got dizzy from the lack of oxygen.

She was still backing out of the room when an icy hand touched her shoulder.

Kate froze, afraid to move. Then she thought better of it and whirled to face whatever—or whoever—had touched her.

"Oh dear, did I frighten you?" Renee said.

She was dressed in black, and Kate assumed that beneath her poufy parka, the photographer's vest with the many pockets was in place. The older woman wore black leather gloves, but her hands were obviously still frozen from the frigid night.

"Just enough to take a dozen or so years off my life," Kate snapped. Renee's sneaking up on her was becoming a bad habit.

She softened her voice. "Actually, I'm glad to see you, Renee. This place is pretty spooky when you think you're alone." She frowned. "Did you just get here? I didn't see your car."

Renee rolled her eyes at the obvious. "It's on the street. Just like I said last time—if we're here to bust the perp, it's wise not to be seen ahead of time. And yes, I got here before you did. I've been casing the joint."

Kate grinned and said, "Good thinking." She didn't bother to remind Renee that "casing the joint" was something thieves did.

Then she sobered. "You haven't seen Sybil, have you?"

Renee shook her head.

"She was supposed to meet me here tonight." Kate glanced around, the spooky, eerie feeling creeping up her spine again. "The strange thing is that the front door was unlocked. That tells me she's here someplace."

"Unless she forgot to lock it when she left. Her car's not here, which tells us she probably isn't either."

Kate agreed, but she couldn't shake the feeling that something didn't add up.

"You packing heat?" Renee had unzipped her parka and was fishing around in her vest for something.

"Packing heat?"

"Carrying a firearm."

"Goodness no. I don't know the first thing about them."

"I figured if ever there was a time we might need it, that time would be now," Renee said. "One of us should be armed."

"You aren't, I hope."

"No. But I stopped by the Mercantile to pick up some other essentials this afternoon." She pulled out two walkie-talkies and handed one to Kate. Next, she patted the multitude of vest pockets, reached in one of them, and pulled out two canisters. Again, she handed one to Kate and tucked the other one back in her pocket.

"Pepper spray," she said. "Next best thing to packing heat."

She showed Kate all the bells and whistles on the walkie-talkies and then disappeared around the corner so they could test their connection.

After a few minutes, Renee's staticky voice warbled, "Think we need backup? Or are we ready to roll? Over and out."

"I think we're ready to roll," Kate responded into the transmitter.

"Ten-four," Renee said, then headed back around the corner to stand in front of Kate.

"We need to cover two areas," Kate said.

She told Renee about the service entrance in the back of the hotel and about the dumbwaiter, which she'd seen on the hotel map originated in a storage area behind the Bristol kitchen and connected to the laundry room upstairs.

"Dumbwaiter?" Renee looked skeptical. "What's that got to do with anything?"

Kate smiled. "I suspect it has a lot to do with everything."

"Like what?"

Kate sighed. "I'll tell you when I figure it out myself."

Renee let out a harrumph.

Kate noticed the moaning wind and icy rain beating against the hotel's windows. She didn't relish the idea of keeping vigil in such weather. Even more, she didn't want Renee to be exposed to the frigid temperatures and blasting wind.

"How about if you keep an eye on the dumbwaiter downstairs?"

Renee nodded, then narrowed her eyes. "You wouldn't be coddling me, would you?"

"Coddling? I wouldn't think of it," Kate said and shot a prayer heavenward, asking forgiveness for the fib. "Let's get started. I'll show you the dumbwaiter."

Renee put on her miner's headlamp and fastened the chin strap. At Kate's quizzical look, she said, "I borrowed it from my mother." Why her ninety-something-year-old mother had a miner's headlamp was a mystery to Kate.

Renee flicked the light on.

Kate pulled her penlight out of her handbag, and with the two dancing beams lighting their way, they crept across the foyer to the Bristol. They let themselves into the kitchen, crossed the polished tile floors, past gleaming stainless-steel appliances, to the storage area behind the restaurant. The service entrance was just beyond.

Kate gestured toward a small ordinary-looking cupboard in the corner near the service entrance.

"That's the dumbwaiter," she whispered. "You need to stay hidden in the shadows and call me if anyone comes in or goes out."

Renee nodded and turned off the miner's lamp. "So, where will you be?"

"The parking lot. I want to see if our 'ghost' appears when there's no audience."

"Good thinking," Renee whispered. "BOLO," she added.

Kate searched her memory bank for the acronym. Then she smiled. "Be on the lookout. You too."

Kate headed to the door and reached for the knob. An eerie moan came from somewhere in the hotel. It was so faint that at first, Kate thought she'd imagined it.

Then the sound carried toward them again, even stronger than before.

"Did you hear that?" Renee whispered, leaving her hiding place. "It sounds like a ghost."

The moan carried toward them again.

Kate aimed her penlight at the dumbwaiter. "It's coming from there."

Renee's eyes grew wide. "You're not going to open it, are you? I mean, right here, without backup or anything? What if there's a body . . ." She shuddered.

Kate went over to the door that made up the exterior of the small elevator. She pushed one of three buttons to the right of the dumbwaiter, and a mechanism inside groaned and coughed and creaked. The unearthly moaning grew louder.

Renee crept closer, dropped her voice, and whispered, "Are you sure you want to do th—"

There was a whirring sound, a small thump, then the thing came to a halt.

Kate took a deep breath and pressed her index finger on the button that said OPEN DOOR.

Chapter Twenty-Six

The dumbwaiter door slowly slid open, and Kate aimed the beam of her penlight flash at the contents.

"Laundry," Renee said. "Can you believe that? It's a pile of laundry. Here, I thought we were about to dis—"

The pile of laundry moved and let out another soft moan.

Kate gently reached into the elevator and, with Renee's help, pulled Sybil into the room.

She blinked at them, her eyes dark with fear. Her mouth was duct-taped. So were her wrists.

Renee pulled some small scissors from her vest and went to work on the tape.

Sybil rubbed her wrists and took a deep breath. "I was hoping you'd hear me," she finally said. "I didn't know how else I'd be found."

"How did this happen?" Kate kept the beam of her flashlight slightly to one side of Sybil's face, so she wouldn't be blinded.

"I honestly don't know. After you called to tell me your suspicions, I came in here to look around. I opened the dumbwaiter, spotted some food that was obviously being sent upstairs, and that's the last thing I remember." She rubbed her head. "Someone must have conked me a good one, because I didn't wake up until I was inside the thing." She grimaced. "Not a comfortable place to be for any length of time, believe me."

"Did you hear voices?"

"No, nothing."

"The perp knows we're onto him," Renee said. "We've got to move fast."

"Wait a minute," Kate said. "This tells us that there's an accomplice. Because the food was sent up alone, instead of taken by hand, I suspect the accomplice was the sender. Our suspect was upstairs in the laundry room waiting."

"Which means?" Sybil rubbed her temple and winced.

"That the perp's thinking he'd better get out of here while the getting's good. He may be armed and dangerous." Renee patted her pockets as if checking for a weapon.

Kate studied Sybil. "Are you okay enough to help us?"

She nodded. "I wouldn't miss this for the world."

"I wonder if the ghost will head for the creek, just like always," Renee said, dropping her voice to a whisper. "We've obviously deduced that the perp and the ghost are one and the same."

"Actually, that's not a certainty," Kate said.

The other two looked at her quizzically, but she didn't explain. There would be time for that later.

"But back to the dumbwaiter. If whoever's upstairs thinks Sybil is still in the dumbwaiter, it will be avoided. So will this back entrance."

"And we can jump him when he heads to the creek," Renee added.

"Why are you so certain that whoever it is will head to the creek?" Sybil said.

Renee harrumphed. "A matter of deduction. The small rowboat, oars, and spent candles were the first clue. Downstream where the water is swift enough and wide enough to accommodate a rowboat."

Sybil arched a brow. "I'm impressed."

Renee threw her head back and sniffed. "I watch a lot of *CSI*."

Kate rummaged through the kitchen cupboards until she found some linens. She wadded them up and piled them in the dumbwaiter with the other linens, then she hit the button to close the door and position it between floors, just as it had been before.

She gave the other women a nod, and then the three stepped out into the freezing rain. They moved gingerly across the ice-slick parking lot, huddling close to keep warm.

Around them, the biting wind gusted and blasts of sleet hit their faces.

"Think about poor Precious McFie," Sybil said. "She walked this path in her wedding gown in the same kind of weather."

"I can't imagine doing that because I was jilted by someone I loved," Renee said. "I can't imagine doing that at all."

"Maybe her fiancé was all she had to live for," Sybil said.

Her voice was sad, and Kate wondered if she was thinking about her own life. She'd once said that the hotel was her whole life, and yet just a few days prior, she was ready to walk away from it. What would that have left her?

"Well, I never . . ." Renee breathed.

Kate and Sybil turned to follow her gaze.

In the upstairs wing, a small light flickered in the window of the dusty unused room, then it moved to the next unused room, then it seemed to hover and stop in the room where Kate had discovered the slipper print.

Renee gasped. "Look at that, will you? The ghost is back!" Her voice was shaking. "And it's real."

Chapter Twenty-Seven

A smoky, veiled figure seemed to float from one window to the next and back again, almost as if dancing. At the same time, a blast of wind, stronger than before, rolled across the parking lot, and the parking lot lights flickered, dimmed, then went out completely. The hotel went black, except for the flickering lights in the upstairs windows.

Sybil groaned. "Ghost or no ghost, I'm getting pretty tired of this."

"I am too," Kate said. She glanced at Renee, smiled, and said, "Let's roll."

But Renee held up a hand to stop her. "Wait," she said. "There are *two* ghosts now."

Kate looked back. In the ambient light through the windows, she could see that the first figure had been joined by another. The first appeared to be female; the second was obviously male. The build, the height . . .

"Ghosts," Renee breathed. "I still say they're ghosts."

They watched for a moment in silence.

Kate caught her breath as two hunched-over figures slipped around the side of the building, arms wrapped around each other, clutching their dark coats close against the wind.

They made their way toward the creek, with no wary glances around, with no apparent concern about being seen.

Something was wrong.

Kate blinked, watching them with narrowed eyes.

They were too nonchalant for the kind of mission they were on. Too cocky. Too perfect.

"They're decoys," she hissed to Renee and Sybil. "That whole ghost business in the windows was a show put on for the benefit of anyone who might be watching."

Sybil and Renee were still watching the couple make their way to the creek.

"We've got to split up," Kate whispered. "You two follow that couple. Find out what you can."

"Where are you going?" Renee asked.

"Back to the service entrance, just to keep an eye on things."

Without another word, Kate pulled up the collar of her coat, and holding the hood close over her head, she trotted back across the dark, icy parking lot to the service entrance.

She arrived just as the door pushed open slowly and there he was. Even in the darkness, she recognized the man exiting the hotel as Newt Keller. She faded back into some brush and held her breath as he swung the beam of his flashlight around. Then, silently, he made his way around beyond the rear of the hotel.

Kate followed, not daring to flip on her own flashlight. She strained to see the objects on the ground in front of her.

If she tripped, the man would hear her and know he was being followed. Worse, she might hurt herself, and at her age, she could ill afford breaking any bones.

The dark figure stayed close to the hotel until he reached the side by the creek, then he cut through some dense brush and disappeared.

Kate stopped, breathing hard from the exertion. Her heart was pounding so hard her ribs moved with each beat. She put her hand to her heart and willed it to slow down to a normal rate.

She almost laughed. It was asking a lot of a heart to chase a suspect through unfamiliar terrain at midnight in an ice storm.

Taking a deep breath, she tried to get her bearings. Where had he disappeared to? And how could she follow if all she could see was darkness all around her? She strained to see a flicker from his flashlight, but either he had turned it off, or the brush was so dense she couldn't see it. She assessed her choices. She could continue feeling her way along with her feet in the dark, or she could flip on her flashlight and charge into the brush, hoping to surprise Newt. That was, supposing he was there. Neither option brought her much comfort.

That's when she heard voices ahead. She halted, listened for a moment, then crept forward inch by agonizingly slow inch.

She had just lifted her foot to take another step when she was hit in the face with a blast of light. She held her hand up to shade her eyes.

"What are you doing out here?" a voice growled.

She blinked as her eyes tried to focus. "Move your light, and I'll tell you," she said. She reached into her pocket to retrieve her flashlight.

"I wouldn't do that if I were you," Newt said, moving closer. The light still blinded her.

"I was just reaching for my flashlight," she said.

He studied her for a moment, then said, "Don't even think about it."

She breathed a quick prayer and, trying not to be detected, moved her hand agonizingly slow, toward her flashlight. She remembered the pepper spray. It would come in handy now, if she could get to it as well, but she didn't want to push her luck.

"You're supposed to be missing. And hurt," she said.

Newt Keller laughed. "Oh yeah, that."

"My friend has been accused of abducting you."

"Actually, I was sorry about the way it turned out. She actually walked right into my plan, and once the police made the connection, I just let it happen."

"Because she saw you at the creek?"

"Yes. She followed me out there and gave me what-for because of how I treat people. We had a scuffle, I cut myself, and well, the rest is history."

He laughed again. "It was supposed to be another ghost story—haven't you figured that out? What a convenient time to rev up the Precious McFie story, add mine to it, boost ratings, and create an atmosphere of suspense. Slipping around the hotel at night, grabbing a snack from the kitchen by candle-light, all so easily explained. A producer's dream."

"All for publicity," Kate said.

He stared at her for a moment. "That's show biz," he said. "Now, if you'll excuse me. I have a boat to catch."

"Oh no, you don't," said a voice behind Kate.

She whirled to see Renee gingerly picking her way along the rough terrain. She was breathing hard with the exertion and put her hand to her chest to catch her breath when she reached them.

"What now?" Keller growled. "As I was saying, I'd love to stay and chat, ladies, but really, I must go."

"Maybe you didn't hear me," Renee said. "You're not going anywhere."

He started to back into the brush. "You can't stop me."

"Maybe this will," Renee said. In one swift movement, she swung her camera to her eye and snapped a picture.

Newt Keller just laughed. "That won't prove anything. With Photoshop, anybody can tamper with a photograph."

Kate took a step toward him. "You're probably right about that. But this little gem?" She fished around in her pocket for the walkie-talkie and held it up. "It's recorded every word you just said to me." She grinned at Renee. "Glad you got the one with all the bells and whistles."

"Give that to me!" He lunged for the unit, but Kate did some fancy footwork, and he missed, only to trip and fall facedown in the mud.

"You're going to the hoosegow," Renee said, standing over him, her foot planted on the small of his back. "I hope for a long, long time after what you've put this town through. What with the fake haunting on top of everything else, likely to scare our townsfolk to death."

He struggled to get up, but before he could right himself, Renee gave him a quick shot of pepper spray. He fell again into the mud, Renee's foot again anchored to his back.

His face in the icy mud, Newt mumbled something to the effect that he knew nothing about a fake haunting.

Kate's eyes widened. He knew nothing about the haunting? Her mind took off in a dozen directions, trying to connect those remaining dots. But she would have to work through it tomorrow. For now, all she wanted to do was get home and get warm.

"Did you call 911?" she asked Renee.

"I told Sybil to when I ran after you."

Newt struggled again to get up, but Renee kept her foot atop the man's back. She continued chatting with Kate as if he were nothing more than a lump of laundry. Very cold and muddy laundry.

A lump of laundry that kept insisting he had nothing to do with the haunting of the hotel.

WITHIN MINUTES, Deputy Spencer drove away with a hand-cuffed Newt Keller in the back of the black-and-white, and Sybil went back into her office to call her corporate head-quarters with the news.

When Kate and Renee reached Kate's Honda, Renee said, "How did you figure out how to use the recorder on the walkie-talkie? I didn't even know it had one."

Kate opened her car door. "Want a ride to your car?"

Renee nodded and climbed in the passenger side.

"I made that up," Kate said. "I didn't know whether it had a recorder."

They both chuckled all the way to Renee's car.

Chapter Twenty-Eight

Kate sat with her Copper Mill friends in the studio audience, relishing the buzz of excitement that seemed to touch everyone around her. It was the final taping for the Taste Network's on-location shoot, as well as the final taping of *Grits 101*. And it was the first time since Susannah's release that she was once again part of the taping.

"I'll miss that little French gal," Joe Tucker said from the row behind Kate. His Groucho impression had never been better.

"I'm glad we've moved on to grits," Caroline muttered.

"Most TV personalities are airheads. But this cute little director Daryl Gallagher sure has done a good job, stepping in as she did," Millie Lovelace said. "It's like she was born for it."

"She'll go places," Eli Weston said. "She may be sweet and cute, but she's got ambition. I can see it in her eyes."

"Nothing like her mother," LuAnne said. "As far as being sweet, I mean. Her mother's so cold, she'd break like an icicle in a windstorm. How could a woman like that raise a warmhearted daughter?"

Kate turned back to watch the preparations for *Grits 101*. At her feet, Kisses growled from his designer tote and Renee bent down to calm him. Kate noticed Renee's questioning glance. Kisses had a tendency to growl in just that manner before the appearance of a ghost, or rather, the onset of gas.

Livvy leaned over to speak to both Renee and Kate. "How do you feel now that the excitement is over? You two are quite the heroes of Copper Mill."

"It's not over," Kate said.

Renee looked surprised. "We took down the perp. What else is there?"

"I just have this feeling," she began as Renee and Livvy exchanged worried glances. "There are too many unanswered questions."

Renee looked around, then lowered her voice. "You mean there's another perp out there?"

Kate nodded. "Too many things don't add up."

"You're still in danger, then," Livvy whispered. "I thought it was over."

Kate pondered that for a moment. The feeling of imminent peril had been growing the past few days. She couldn't pinpoint why; she just knew it was there.

The audience hushed as Daryl Gallagher came running in with a wide smile. She was back to her pep-girl persona and seemed ready to break into a cheer as she revved up the audience for the show.

"First of all," she said, "in the event that you haven't heard, Newt Keller has been found alive and well." There was polite applause from the studio audience, and a smattering of groans from the Taste crew onstage.

She then turned to the three celebrity chefs standing in
the wings and motioned them out. As Daryl waxed eloquent
about their contributions to *Celebrity Chefs of the South*, Kate
sat back and frowned. Why had there been no mention that
Newt Keller's abduction was a hoax? Or Nicolette's role in it?

No one else seemed to notice, and Kate went back to
watching the three chefs interact as if there'd never been any
tension among them. These women, as stellar as their cooking skills were, were also incredibly adept actors. Especially
Susannah, who bantered and smiled with Nicolette, Birdie,
Daryl, and the audience.

The *Grits 101* taping continued without a hitch. Daryl
was in fine form with her combined talents of revving up the
studio audience and demanding excellence from the chef and
crew. She had fit into the role of director like Cinderella's foot
in the glass slipper.

As soon as the taping was over, Daryl again stepped in
front of the audience. "You may have heard rumors already
about this, but we at Taste Network are joining forces with
the Bristol to throw a Western-style barbecue for you all." She
gave them more details about the time and place—the hotel
parking lot, weather permitting. "At any rate, we'll have the
grills up and running by two o'clock, and run them until
we close down after dark. Everyone in town is invited, and
there will be no charge. It's just our way of saying thank you
for letting us take over your town for as long as we have.

"Meantime, we have some final shoots to take care of during the next few days, some special segments about the hotel,
especially its interesting history, plus a feature on some of the

unique characters who've stayed here through the years. So if you see us around town, you'll know what we're up to."

Kate stood and clapped with the rest of the audience, then she hurried down the risers to talk with Susannah.

She halted midstep when she saw Nicolette huddle with her daughter. The two had moved slightly away from the others, then continued to move toward the swinging doors of the Bristol kitchen.

Everyone else in the studio audience was chatting or otherwise distracted. Kate glanced around to make sure no one noticed, then followed the mother-daughter duo at a distance.

She stepped toward the back of the studio kitchen set and moved as close as she dared to the cardboard-thin faux kitchen wall. Though the two women spoke in low tones, she could hear every word.

"I need to borrow your phone," Nicolette said.

"What's wrong with yours?" Gone was the sunny cheerleader persona. In its place was barely contained anger.

"Look, honey, I know you're upset with what happened. I couldn't tell you. I didn't want you to get involved."

A short, bitter laugh erupted from Daryl. "You think I didn't know what you and Newt had planned?"

There was a moment of silence, then Nicolette said, "You knew?"

"Of course I knew. I'm not stupid, Mother. I overheard you two scheming months ago. I knew every bit of it, start to finish. It all worked out perfectly for me."

"Because it gave you a chance to show off your star power to the execs, including your new 'best friend,' Jacqueline

Keller? I wondered how you moved into that role with such ease."

"Think what you will, but you wouldn't understand anyway. You never have understood me. Or maybe I should say, you've never made the effort."

"Understand what?"

"Here's the phone, Mother." The last word dripped with sarcasm. "You're welcome to it, but you'll have to talk fast. The battery is almost dead."

Kate faded back into the studio audience, then turned just as Nicolette strode from the studio, the cell phone in her hand. Kate followed just long enough to see her punch in some numbers, listen for a dial tone, shake the phone, punch numbers in again, then finally flip the phone closed.

As a parting shot to her daughter, instead of returning the cell, she tossed it in a rather elegant trash receptacle by the service exit.

As soon as the woman had walked outside to the parking lot, Kate dove for the trash receptacle. She found the phone immediately, resting atop some paper napkins.

She flipped it open. The tiny battery icon was almost empty. The phone would go dead within seconds. With trembling fingers, she tapped the buttons to access the text-message files, those sent and those received.

She saw just a glimpse of what she was looking for before the phone went dead. She had the strange sensation she was being watched. She turned as Daryl Gallagher stepped from the hotel entrance.

"Is that my phone?" Gone was the smile, the bouncy pep girl. Kate looked into her eyes and saw stark fear.

"I-I saw your mother drop it," Kate said. "I went to retrieve it."

"It's mine, not hers." Daryl yanked the phone from Kate's grasp. "You flipped it open."

There was something about her petite figure, the way she moved as she stepped closer, the ballerina stance, the hint of a demiplié that was familiar. Again she remembered taking her daughters to their ballet lessons. The lessons only lasted one hour a week for six weeks, but Kate still remembered the foot positions and a few of the terms. The girls had practiced at home for months, long after the lessons were over.

"Why did you flip it open if you saw my mother drop it?"

"I . . . I—"

"Yoo-hoo," Susannah sang out as she rolled her suitcase out of the hotel. Though she had moved her coach to the Hanlons' earlier, she'd left some of her belongings in the hotel.

Kate smiled with relief and gave her friend a wave. "Are you packed and ready to go?"

Susannah nodded. "I hate to leave. Our friendship has come to mean so much to me all over again." She looked at Daryl. "I want you to know how proud I am of you. You've done a stellar job filling in the way you did. Everybody's saying so. Congratulations."

Daryl turned red, mumbled her thanks, then quickly skittered off.

Kate and Susannah continued making their way across the parking lot to the Miata. It was parked next to the *Sumptuous Chocolates* star coach. Susannah rummaged through her purse for her keys.

"Well, dear friend, this is about it," she said.

Kate started to give her a hug, then remembered the stained-glass votive. "Oh dear, I almost forgot. I made something for you. Wait here."

She trotted across the parking lot to the Honda, clicked open the trunk, and lifted out a carefully padded and wrapped cardboard box. She carried it over to Susannah.

"My goodness," Susannah said. "Can I open it here?"

Kate nodded. "I'd love that."

But before she could unwrap the package, the whining roar of a motorcycle heading into the parking lot caught their attention.

Kate blinked in surprise as it rounded the first row of cars, then the second, and finally the third. It was as if the driver was looking for a specific car. Or person.

Then, as if in slow motion, the motorcycle careened toward where Kate and Susannah stood.

Susannah screamed as the driver put the vehicle into a sideways slide and skidded into them.

Kate's scream caught in her throat as she was slammed against the Miata, then tumbled to the ground. Susannah crumbled like a rag doll beside her.

The driver was dressed in black leather, and his face was covered by the dark visor of his helmet. He revved the engine, spun around the parking lot once more, then skidded by the two women again and lobbed a heavy object at Kate. It clunked against her temple, and she fell backward, tumbling into deep black velvet nothingness.

Kate groaned as she came to then touched her head to see if there was any blood. She winced. No blood, but a goose egg was already forming.

"You okay?" she whispered shakily to Susannah. Her voice came out in a hoarse whisper. She tried to stand, but her shaking legs wouldn't support her.

"I don't think anything is broken. How about you?" Susannah said weakly as she pulled herself to standing. She hobbled over to Kate, and helped her up.

By then, people were streaming out of the hotel and running toward them. Someone shouted "Call 911!"

"Did the package break?" Kate asked Susannah.

But Susannah wasn't listening. She had picked up the fist-size rock that hit Kate. It was crudely wrapped with a piece of paper and bound by a large rubberband.

Susannah unwrapped it, read the message, then handed it to Kate. "I'm not leaving until this is settled," she said.

Kate's knees turned to rubber again as she read the message scrawled in large black felt-tip letters: IT ISN'T OVER YET.

Chapter Twenty-Nine

I'm worried about you, Kate," Paul said at breakfast. "I'll be glad when the network folks are out of town."

"I think a lot of people will agree with you, but for entirely different reasons. They just want their town back." Kate laughed lightly. "I'll be glad for all the others to leave, but I do wish Susannah could stay around for a while. After the rock was thrown at me, she moved right back into the hotel."

Kate pondered her memories for a moment, then said, "The day the sheriff drove her away in the back of his SUV, the past came rushing back to me. Susannah truly became part of our family. I guess in a way, I'd like to recapture that. We were as close as sisters."

"That's why you were willing to risk your life to clear her name." Paul reached across the table and squeezed Kate's fingers. "You did an amazing thing, Katie, going after Newt Keller the way you did—"

She laughed and held up a hand. He took a sip of coffee, studying Kate over the rim for a moment.

"About today, Katie," he said solemnly. "I've been watching you puzzling out the last few pieces to the mystery. Something tells me you've got something up your sleeve for the cookout."

She patted his hand. "As I said, you know me well."

"This is no lighthearted matter, Kate."

"I know. There are just a few puzzle pieces missing that I still need to work out. I just don't know how they fit."

"Such as . . . ?"

"The ghost of Precious McFie."

"You don't think Newt Keller was behind all that haunted hotel business?"

"It's someone else, but the motive eludes me."

"What are the other missing pieces?"

"Susannah's stolen recipe, the shenanigans in her studio kitchen, the fact that someone seems out to get her, and the fact that someone still seems out to get me too."

"Do you think all these pieces are connected?"

"Yes, but I don't know how." She stood to refill their coffee mugs.

"Promise me you won't step out of my sight tonight."

Kate grinned. "The whole town will be there, plus all the network people. I can't imagine anyone attempting anything dangerous with such a large audience."

Paul sighed. "I suppose you're right. Just promise me you won't put yourself in danger."

She ruffled his hair and bent down to kiss him. "I'll try," she said, and Paul just shook his head.

She had only one thing on her mind in preparation for the

cookout, and it wasn't what she was going to wear. She sat
down at the computer, typed out a quick e-mail, and sent it
off into cyberspace on a wing and a prayer.

As KATE AND PAUL parked alongside the Hamilton Springs
Hotel, icy fingers of fear crept up her spine. Maybe it was
residual emotion from the peril she'd experienced during her
last two visits to the hotel.

Holding Paul's hand, she tried to act as normal as possible
as they made their way through the gathering crowd, stopping
to visit with friends and parishioners and network people.
Large metal barbecues had been brought in, and the smoky
scent of grilled chicken and steak hung in the air. Tables had
been set up, complete with red-and-white-checked plastic
cloths.

The afternoon was balmy and, for early December, unsea-
sonably warm. Maybe it was just that it was such a contrast
to the recent winter storms.

In her experience, she'd figured out that suspects who
excelled at cat-and-mouse games loved nothing better than
baiting the mouse, playing with it until it tired, then going in
for the kill, mostly figuratively, but sometimes literally. She
hoped it would be the former.

She hadn't told Paul her plan because she didn't want him
to worry. For her plan to work, she had to do it alone.

She had no weapon except the pepper spray Renee had
given her. Even so, her best weapons were prayer and a quick
mind. She worried about being quick enough; fright could
sometimes dull her senses. But she knew that God wouldn't
fail her.

Kate spotted Susannah and excused herself from the group she and Paul had stopped to visit with.

"I can't tell you why," she said to Susannah, "but if I'm not back in ten minutes, alert Paul. Tell him to call the sheriff."

Susannah frowned. "What are you up to?"

Kate patted her arm. "Just a little game of cat and mouse." She let out a nervous laugh. "Actually, more appropriately, I think I'm about to bell the cat."

Susannah didn't laugh with her. "You're the mouse, then. The prey. Kate, you can't do this. I'll go with you."

"No, Suse. It won't work if you go with me. I've got this final piece of the puzzle to put together, and I intend to do it today."

Susannah started to say something else, but Kate was off and running. She skirted around the edges of a few groups, called out greetings to Livvy and Danny, waved to Renee and Caroline, and smiled at a dozen other friends, making sure she was a highly visible mouse.

Glancing around, she then moved quickly into the hotel. A few guests were seated in the foyer, and the girl behind the reception desk looked up and smiled.

"Is Sybil in her office?"

"Yes, I believe she is," the girl said.

Kate knocked on the general manager's door and asked if she could borrow the master key card to the spare rooms upstairs.

"You're not still investigating those hauntings, are you?"

Kate nodded. "I'll fill you in later. For now, I just need to check out the upstairs wing."

"Be careful. After what's happened, I've had those three

front rooms taken apart, stem to stern. There's equipment everywhere."

"Workers too?"

"Oh no, not on the weekend. But they left their ladders, sanders, crowbars, drills, buckets of paint; you name it, it's there." She laughed. "I want that whole area aired out, revamped, and put to good use. I don't want a hint of haunting ever to be linked with this hotel again."

"Good thinking," Kate said, taking the key card.

"I'll walk with you to the foyer," Sybil said. "I'm not about to miss that cookout."

As they headed into the foyer, Sybil invited the front desk clerk and the guests to join her outside.

Kate was alone in the hotel. Again. And she didn't know if the cat was following its prey.

She approached the staircase, put her foot on the bottom stair, clutched the handrail, and took a deep breath.

Chapter Thirty

K ate ignored her thumping heart and headed up the stairs to the unoccupied wing of the hotel. She paused to listen for footsteps behind her, which would tell her that the trap was set. But because of the hallway runner, sounds were easily muffled. She probably couldn't even hear the squeak of a shoe.

The overhead light was dim, which gave the long hallway a ghostly, eerie feeling. The pale shadows of the workers' equipment added to Kate's growing sense of peril. Before, the hallway was empty, and she knew she was alone. Now, there were places to hide, and she didn't know anything for certain.

She wet her lips and forced herself to walk to the first door, pass the key card through the lock, and open it. A tarp covered the floor, with several buckets of paint resting on top, and two ladders were set up at opposite sides of the room.

She stepped back into the hall and glanced around.

The cat hadn't taken the bait. Yet.

She checked the contents of the second room. It was in the same state of disrepair as the first.

Again, she waited for the sounds of someone coming toward the wing.

There was nothing.

Kate opened the laundry-room door. It too was about to get a new coat of paint. She turned to leave.

That's when she heard footsteps. But before she could react, the overhead lights in the hallway went out. The darkness seemed so dense, it made her worry about breathing.

"So you followed me after all," Kate said.

Daryl laughed. "Did you really think I was stupid enough to fall for your little act? I didn't follow you here; I came to carry out my threats."

"Ah, yes, the threats," Kate said. "You looked pretty scared when you saw me with your phone. Until I saw those messages, you might have fooled me. But it was your graceful ballerina walk that cinched it, and the ballet slipper prints."

She forced awe into her voice. "Since you wanted me to stop investigating, I surmised you're the Hamilton Springs ghost. It all makes sense."

"My, my, you are smart," Daryl said. "I suppose since you'll be suffering a terrible fall soon, I can divulge my, shall we say, antics."

"You were very good at them," Kate said. "You almost had me convinced." She paused, playing for time. "How did you know I'd figured out it was you?"

"I wasn't sure until you picked up my phone—though I'd been watching you since I ran into you up here, that day you tried to hide from my mother and me. The texts were just insurance to get you off my back."

"How did you do it, the ghostly dances, the haunting?"

Daryl laughed again. "I can't take full credit. It helps that my boyfriend designs props for magic shows."

"And drives a motorcycle."

"That too."

"Why, Daryl, when you have so much going for you?"

"Ratings are everything. Haven't you figured that out? And your flying leap from the second floor of this old, haunted hotel will catapult me further into the national media spotlight." She chuckled, and in the abject darkness, the sound was hollow. Sinister. "The question is, why did you come up here tonight? Why did you give me the opportunity I needed to help you take that delightful dive into the night?"

"Don't you know that criminals always return to the scene of the crime?"

"As we say in the biz, that's cliché. I'm disappointed. Couldn't you come up with a better reason than that?"

Kate shrugged and forced nonchalance into her voice. "And I'd hoped to reason with you."

Daryl let out a shrill laugh. "You've got to be kidding. What in heaven's name for?"

"Maybe because of heaven's name," Kate said quietly. "Maybe because just as God never gives up on us, we shouldn't give up on each other. I've seen how your mother watches you when you're not looking. There's pride in her eyes. And love. Maybe you haven't noticed, but it's there."

Daryl fell quiet for a moment, and Kate thought maybe she'd touched something long buried in the young woman's heart.

She was wrong. "It's time for you step out on the window ledge," Daryl said. "And if you doubt that I can make you do it, you might consider this." She stuck what felt like a revolver against Kate's back.

She blinked. "You can't be serious. In front of all the guests?"

"Do I look that stupid? Of course not. Your accident will happen in the infamous room 213, which faces the creek. I'll do a few more ghostly pirouettes in the usual windows, and you'll go down in the newspaper accounts as yet another tragedy caused by the ghost of Precious McFie."

She pushed Kate down the hallway toward the room, unlocked the door with a key card of her own, and shoved Kate inside. She stepped inside right after Kate and locked the door behind her.

"I know why you did this," Kate said, hoping to play for time.

But Daryl gave her a little push toward the window. "Yeah, I'm sure you do."

"You decided to help your mother and Newt Keller when you figured out what they were up to. So you came a few weeks early to play the role of the Hamilton Springs ghost."

"How do you know that?"

"I checked the guest list at reception. You may have thought you were being very clever using a fictitious name, but a signature comparison was fairly easy to come by."

"So what if I did come early? Maybe I was here to check out the facilities before the network people arrived."

"The sightings escalated, then continued each time you slipped in for another stay."

"You can't prove the connection."

"I think any jury would easily get the picture."

"So what exactly have I done that's illegal? Impersonate a ghost? That's a laugh."

"Threatening me with a gun is a good start," Kate said. She breathed a prayer, hoping above all that Susannah had alerted Paul, and he'd found the sheriff in the crowded parking lot. "Sending threatening text messages is a crime as well. And I don't need to mention breaking and entering and stealing recipes from Susannah Applebaum's unpublished book."

"That's a good one. You have no proof. Who would believe you?"

"The proof is in the missing ingredient, my dear. The question is why . . . though I think I know the answer to that too."

"What missing ingredient?"

"Susannah told me she leaves out a key ingredient in all her unpublished recipes. They're added at the last minute. Ingenious, don't you think?" She paused. "It was the missing ingredient that told me you were my prime suspect."

"How can that be?"

"The missing ingredient was so obvious. Your mother picked up on it right away and adjusted the recipe. I watched you the day your mother taped that segment. You were upset when she asked for someone to bring her a cup of fresh-brewed, strong coffee."

"Coffee?"

"The missing ingredient."

Before Daryl could answer, the sound of approaching footsteps in the hallway reached them.

Daryl scowled. "If anyone comes close, you're going out the window. So don't think about calling for help."

"So far none of your crimes is serious. But murder is something else entirely," Kate said, trying to keep her voice from shaking. She ventured a glance toward the window, trying not to think about the distance to the hard, rocky ground below.

A knock sounded at the door. "Daryl, are you in there?" The voice was soft, with a French accent. "Daryl? I've been looking all over for you. I saw the gun in your handbag earlier, and I'm worried about you. Please, let's talk."

In the instant that Nicolette distracted her daughter, Kate took her chance and lunged at the gun in Daryl's hand. She grabbed Daryl's forearm and held on for dear life with both her hands. The only thing she could think of was keeping the thing pointed away from them both. And the door.

They scuffled, breathing hard. The gun dropped, and Kate went for it. But Daryl was faster. She stepped on Kate's hand, splaying it out flat above the gun with a crunch. Kate bit back a yelp.

Kate got up and pushed Daryl as hard as she could. The younger woman toppled over, and Kate leaped for the door and unlocked it with one hand and reached for the light switch with the other.

Nicolette stood in the darkened doorway, staring at her daughter. She stared at the gun Daryl had grabbed when Kate went for the door. "Why . . . ?"

For a moment, no one spoke.

"I think she's trying to get your attention," Kate said quietly.

Both women turned to her, looking surprised, as if they'd forgotten she was there.

"What do you mean?" Nicolette said to Kate. Then she scowled at her daughter. "Give me that." She took the gun away from Daryl and held it gingerly away from her body as if it were a snake ready to strike.

"Your daughter has been working behind the scenes, trying to make you the star of the Taste Network, trying to increase the ratings of an already popular show."

"You can't prove that," Daryl growled. "I haven't done anything wrong."

"What about the tiramisu recipe you stole?"

"That's an old family recipe . . ." Daryl began.

"You said your grandmother gave it to you when you were in Italy last summer." Nicolette hesitated. "Daryl, what she's saying? Is there any truth to it?"

Daryl shrugged.

"You can ask Susannah," Kate said. She locked her gaze on Daryl's eyes. "We've already discussed the proof. But what about the other shenanigans you pulled in Susannah's studio kitchen in an attempt to trip her up?"

Daryl shrugged. "I just wanted to level the playing field."

"You almost ruined her career," Kate said.

Nicolette gaped at her daughter. "You did all these things?" She frowned. "Why?"

"You once told me Susannah was your biggest obstacle to

becoming number one in our network. You said you wished you could be rid of her ever-smiling face. I was only trying to help."

"I wasn't serious, Daryl. How could you think such a thing?"

"Easy. When you started getting chummy with Newt Keller, I figured you were trying to help your placement in the lineup. I mean, really, Mother, how could anyone care for such an insensitive boor? I figured it was all an act. I wanted to help you along, that's all."

"We care about each other, but that's beside the point. And we meant for Newt's disappearance to be a simple publicity stunt. Then it was as if someone struck a match to dry timber. The whole thing turned into a nightmare." She stared at her daughter.

"I was just trying to help you ... to help us all. I gave you everything, every advantage a mother could give a child." Her voice quavered, and she stared at her daughter as if she were seeing her for the first time. "You disappeared a few weeks before the network arrived here. You were strangely absent when the ghost of Precious McFie danced in front of the hotel windows. There was a ballet-slipper print...your years in dance ..." She stared at her daughter in disbelief. "Tell me that wasn't you."

Daryl laughed. "I do have to admit those were some of my finer moments. The candles, the dancing in the windows with a filmy gown and wedding veil I picked up at a thrift shop. Leaving the print on the dusty table."

"Newt fell for it," Nicolette said.

THE MISSING INGREDIENT   225

"That part was better than playing the role of Precious McFie. Can you imagine the laughs we had over that?"

"We?"

"You know Craig. My boyfriend? Or did you pay any attention when I introduced you?"

"He had a bad fall recently, didn't he?" Kate said, connecting yet another set of dots. "I believe he said he was pushed down the hotel stairs by the ghost, if I'm not mistaken."

Shaking her head as if talking about an errant child, Daryl rolled her eyes. "Honestly, I tried to talk him out of it, but he insisted. Thought it would add some drama." She laughed. "And it did. Really had Sybil going for a while, not to mention all the other folks in town."

Nicolette took two steps closer to her daughter. When she spoke her daughter's name, the sound was filled with heartbreaking disappointment and guilt and no small measure of love. "Oh, Daryl . . ."

"You've always been too busy for me, Mother." Daryl's eyes filled. "Maybe Mrs. Hanlon's right. Maybe all this was in part to get your attention." Her voice dropped, and she sounded like a child when she continued. "Maybe I thought you would love me because I did it all for you."

The muffled sounds of voices carried toward them, growing louder by the second. It was as if all the cookout guests were coming upstairs. Soon the thundering thumps of footsteps grew closer, and Kate could make out the sounds of worried voices.

Kate made a move for the door.

"Stop right there," Daryl said.

When Kate turned, she saw that Daryl had grabbed the gun again. And it was aimed at her.

Nicolette stepped between them. "You'll have to shoot me first," she said quietly.

Kate's heart thumped beneath her ribs, and she swallowed hard.

Daryl kept the gun trained on her mother, then tears filled her eyes, and she dropped the weapon to her side.

Without waiting another heartbeat, Kate ran out into the hallway.

Paul was the first to round the corner, a stream of Copper Mill and Faith Briar friends trotting behind him. She saw Livvy wave, but as soon as Paul reached her, she fell into his arms.

Her eyes were closed, but behind her, she heard the click of handcuffs, then the sound of Sheriff Roberts's voice as he read Daryl Gallagher her rights.

From somewhere in the crowd, a voice called out, "Off to the hoosegow, lady. You shouldn't have been packing heat."

Kate would have known that voice anywhere.

"I thought you promised to be careful," Paul murmured into Kate's ear. She could feel the wild beating of his heart against her cheek. She closed her eyes and savored the moment—the safety of his arms, the warmth of his love, the knowledge that all the dots had at last been connected.

She pulled back and smiled up at him. "How did you know where I was?"

He smiled and nodded toward the windows on the front

side of the hotel. "There was a flickering light. Everyone saw it. It flitted from window to window."

"But we weren't on that side of the hotel," Kate said, inclining her head to room 213. "We were in there, and all the lights were out."

"Strange," Paul said.

"Not strange at all," Renee said, emerging from the crowd to stand beside Paul. From somewhere in the depths of the doggie tote tucked under her arm, Kisses growled.

Renee shot Kate a knowing look and winked.

Epilogue

Susannah's *Sumptuous Chocolates* star coach pulled up in front of Kate and Paul's home on a Saturday the first week in June. Kate ran to the door even before her friend knocked. Paul was just three steps behind her.

The women hugged, then Kate invited her in. "We're delighted you could stop by."

Susannah gave Paul a hug, then smiled at them both. "I wouldn't have missed this for the world. It was just pure luck—" She stopped to correct herself. "No, it was a God thing that put you directly in my path to our next gig. You were on the way, but I would have driven a hundred miles out of the way for this visit."

"Come in and sit down," Paul said, leading the way to the living room. "Would you care for coffee?"

"I'd love some. Kenyan French roast?"

"Italian," Paul said with a chuckle. "By the way, even though it's getting close to summer, we're still enjoying *Chocolaté Dos Mundos*."

Susannah grinned. "It's addictive."

She sat on one end of the sofa, and Kate sat on the other. Paul left them to talk while he put on the coffee.

"How are things going with the book sales?"

"Couldn't be better. And my cookware business has turned around as well. My time here in Copper Mill changed a lot of things. I'll never forget how you helped me through one of the most troubling times in my life. I don't know how I can ever thank you, Kate."

Kate smiled. "That's what friends are for."

"And you reintroduced me to another friend. Half the day, I go around humming 'His Eye Is on the Sparrow' just because this little sparrow"—she tapped her heart—"needs to be reminded that someone is holding her close, even when she doesn't realize it."

Susannah reached into her satchel and pulled out a book. It was *Chocolates to Die For*. She placed both hands on top of it and, for a moment, just looked down as if thinking about what she was going to say next. Or praying. Maybe both.

When she looked up, she had tears in her eyes. She handed the book to Kate. "This is for you."

Kate took the book in her hands. "Thank you. I'll cherish it."

"I mean it's *really* for you."

Kate tilted her head, puzzled.

"Open it, silly," Susannah said, smiling through her tears.

She reached across the sofa and opened the book to the dedication page, then handed the book back to Kate.

Kate's eyes filled as she read:

To Margaret Blume—
You taught me the joys of cooking,
the fun of family life,
the meaning of love and acceptance, without strings
attached.
I will never forget you.
And to Kate—
In the words of Henry Wadsworth Longfellow,
"I breathed a song into the air,
It fell to earth, I knew not where;
For who has sight so keen and strong
That it can follow the flight of song?
Long, long afterward . . .
The song, from beginning to end,
I found again in the heart of a friend."
You helped me find my song, dear Kate,
then and now.

About the Author

DIANE NOBLE is the award-winning author of *The Butterfly Farm* and nearly two dozen other published works—mysteries, romantic suspense, historical fiction, and non-fiction books for women, including three devotionals and an empty-nest survival guide. Diane is a three-time recipient of the Silver Angel Award for Media Excellence and a double finalist for Romance Writers of America's prestigious RITA award for Best Inspirational Fiction. Diane makes her home in Southern California with husband Tom and their two cats. You can stop by Diane's Web site at www.dianenoble.com to catch up on the latest about her books, favorite recipes, crochet patterns, and much more.

Mystery and the Minister's Wife

Through the Fire by Diane Noble
A State of Grace by Traci DePree
A Test of Faith by Carol Cox
The Best Is Yet to Be by Eve Fisher
Angels Undercover by Diane Noble
Where There's a Will by Beth Pattillo
Into the Wilderness by Traci DePree
Dog Days by Carol Cox
A Token of Truth by Sunni Jeffers
The Missing Ingredient by Diane Noble